The Beverly Hoodbillies

Disclaimer:

This is a work of fiction. Names, characters, businesses, places, events and incidents are either the products of the author's imagination or used in a fictitious manner. Any resemblance to actual persons, living or dead, or actual events is purely coincidental.

Step into the lives of Kweeta and Bushwick. They were your average couple living in Watts barely scraping by. Their circumstances change drastically when Kweeta becomes the heir to a wealthy aunt's inheritance. The first order of business, moving out of the hood and preparing for the glow up in Beverly Hills.

As suspected, not everyone is happy about having the pair as their new neighbors. New friendships are made and others fall by the wayside. Tension grows and tempers flare as Kweeta's newly acquired wealth begin to put a strain on her and Bushwick's relationship. Join this comedic thrill ride to find out if their love will stand the test of time.

Chapter 1 – Best Day Ever

"*This is some bullshit,*" Kweeta thought as she slid the dingy mop across the greasy lobby floor. She'd been working at Taco Bell for three years and had nothing to show for it except tired feet and an expanding waistline. Moving up to management and taking on a boat load of stress wasn't worth the measly $1.80 an hour raise.

There was no time to think about being tired. She still had three hours left in her shift and when she got off she had a set of braids to do that night. Her cosmetology license came in handy, helping her make ends meet. Her dream was to save up enough money to eventually open a shop of her own. However, with a kid and bills getting higher each day, she had to put her dreams on hold for the time being. All she knew was there had to be something better than what she was doing on a daily. Sure she managed to do a few heads here and there but the recent boost in women sporting natural styles as well as the lace front craze, put a dent in her funds. Not to mention working full time as a stylist meant she would have to come out of pocket for health care for her and her daughter. As much as she hated this job she did have access to an affordable health plan.

Her thoughts soon moved to her child's father and lover of four years, Bushwick Stewart. An aspiring rapper and all around hustler. The couple met at the local swap meet when she stopped by his booth and picked up one of his mix tapes. Bushwick was a little man with a big heart and an even bigger set of balls when it came to going after what he wanted. Upon meeting him she wasn't initially interested, however he pursued her aggressively till he made her his bae. His drive and ambition would prove to be equally matched by his charismatic charm. Hopefully this would be a day he would slide through and pick her up so she wouldn't have to wait for two busses to get home.

No sooner than she got the thought out of her mind her phone vibrated in her uniform pocket. She discreetly looked at the caller ID. Her face lit up when she saw that it was him. She pushed the mop bucket to the corner and slipped into a bathroom stall to return his call.

"Hey bae wassup?" Kweeta asked when Bushwick picked up.

"Just checking to see if you still getting off at seven? I'm coming to get you."

"Yep, seven on the dot," she giggled. Despite her and Bushwick being together for several years, he still gave her butterflies in her stomach.

"Good, cause I got a surprise for my baby," he replied. "I'm taking you out after work. You know we gotta celebrate me getting off house arrest."

"Aww, bae I'm sorry but you know I gotta do Laronica's hair tonight."

"I just ran into her at the gas station. She said she had to cancel and she would call you later. Plus yo' mama said she would watch Bugatti."

"Alright, well I guess we're on then. I gotta get back on the floor. I'll talk to you later.

"Alright, see you at seven."

Despite the fact the she was going to hang with her boo, Kweeta was a bit disappointed that her sister was canceling out on her. She was depending on that money to pay the cable bill.

As she made her way back behind the counter her phone vibrated again. She stepped into the storage room to answer the text she'd gotten from Laronica.

"Something came up. I gotta cancel."

"Bushwick gave me the message. I gotta get back to work ttyl."

Kweeta knew that this most likely meant Laronica was chasing behind that no good husband of hers. She spent damn near every waking moment trying to catch him and one of his many hoes in the act. And yet she had the nerve to judge her and Bushwick's relationship. She could have said much more but she decided to just let her know that she'd already received the message.

Later that evening

No sooner than Kweeta stepped out the door Bushwick was there waiting for her like clockwork. When she hopped in the car she couldn't help but notice how fine her man was. She thought back to when she first met him she told herself she could never date a man this short. Standing at only 5'4", his head stopped at her voluptuous breast. It was a turn off at first, but after getting to know him she soon realized that Bushwick had the swag of a man twice his height. His smooth walnut complexion and sexy smile still made her weak after all these years. Not to mention the fact that her baby stayed fresh to death.

"Hey boo," she announced before giving him a smack on the lips.

"What up?" Imma run you by the house real quick so you can change. Then it's time to turn up!"

Kweeta was geeked. Her work schedule had been hectic. And it had been a minute since she and Bushwick had stepped out. Since his house arrest they couldn't go anywhere that required him to be out past 6pm, or on the weekends, when he was on 24 hour house arrest. He had gotten caught up in an altercation in the club when a little young punk tried to push up on her and felt on her behind. Little to the other man's knowledge Bushwick was a beast when it came time to knuckle up. He wouldn't hesitate to protect the woman he loved. The dude thought that he was going to get the best of him because of his size. In reality Bushwick beat the breaks off of the guy. In fact he stomped him so bad that he had a concussion and almost died. Luckily he pulled through. Bushwick served his time and was finally getting rid of that ankle bracelet. It was definitely a time to celebrate!

"Hey mama," Kweeta announced when she stepped into the house. "Thanks for watching Bugatti."

"Mhh hmm," Bernisha replied with a slight bit of saltiness to her tone. She was lightweight jealous of the fact that she had no one to take her out.

Since Kweeta's daddy had left her fourteen years ago, the 56 year-old had yet to find someone new. Little to Kweeta's knowledge the only reason she was doing them this favor was because she needed the money, otherwise she really didn't have much time for her granddaughter. She would much rather be playing spades and sipping Moscato with her girls.

"I hope y'all don't plan on staying out all night."

"Now mama you know we ain't staying out that late. I gotta work in the morning."

"I'm glad somebody has to work," Bernisha spat under her breath. For the life of her she couldn't understand what the hell her daughter saw in Bushwick's little short ass. As far as she was concerned he was a wanna be hustler that had nothing to offer her daughter.

Kweeta pretended that she didn't hear her mother's smart ass remark. She wasn't about to let her ruin her evening.

"Hey B."

Kweeta stepped into her eleven year-old's room and kissed her on the forehead.

"How was your day sweetie?"

"It was good," the child replied. You and daddy going out?"

"Yep, we won't be too late. Make sure you finish all your homework and mind your grandma."

"Kweeta, hurry up. I'm starving," Bushwick yelled from the living room."

"Alright! I'm coming, gimme a minute!"

Kweeta took a five-minute shower then stepped into a hot pink, backless jumpsuit she'd just gotten from her favorite hood boutique on Instagram, Pucci Vuittron. She slid her feet into a pair of knock off Fendi stiletto's she picked up from the swap meet. If it were one thing she prided herself on was how to keep her family looking fly for a fraction of the cost. Niggas was out here sporting Saint Laurent jeans when her baby looked just as good in his Savage Laurents

"Shiiid, you can't tell me these don't look like the real thing!" She cooed as she admired how sexy the shoes looked on her feet.

She ran a brush through her forty-inch honey blonde Remy lace front, applied a fresh coat of lipstick, grabbed her bootleg Hermes bag and headed for the front door.

"Damn girl don't hurt nobody wit yo fine ass!" Bushwick called out when she emerged from the bedroom.

"You look pretty mama," Bugatti chimed in.

"Thanks y'all," Kweeta giggled. "You ready baby?"

"Hell yeah, let's roll!" Bushwick replied after checking to make sure he had his Red Lobster coupon in his wallet.

After they were seated and had placed their order Bushwick began confessing his feelings for Kweeta.

"Baby girl, you know I love you right?"

"Of course I do bae. I love you too."

"And you know imma hold us down no matter what?"

"Of course I do baby. You always do. What's this all about?"

"Lemme finish…now you remember I said I had a surprise?"

"Yes," Kweeta replied, squirming in her seat from excitement.

"The first part is I got signed to Holla Back records."

"Oh my God! I'm so happy for you baby!" Kweeta jumped from her seat and wrapped her arms around Bushwick's neck. "I always believed in you."

"I know you did. That brings me to the second half of my surprise. You know we been doin' this thang for a minute now. And you have always had my back through thick and thin. I couldn't ask for a woman more loyal than you."

By now Kweeta looked totally confused.

Bushwick reached in his jacket pocket and pulled out a small box.

Kweeta's eyes lit up.

Bushwick stood from his seat and kneeled down in front of Kweeta's chair, she could feel her eyes getting moist. Everyone who was seated around them held their breath as he made his proposal.

"Oh my God Bushwick, are you serious?" Kweeta sniffled.

"Dead serious, you are my queen and I love you girl. I know you have been wanting this but I wanted to wait till I could take care of you."

"You always take care of me," Kweeta replied softly, looking into his eyes.

"I did ok, but now that I have this gig I can do even better. You and Bugatti are my whole world. I want to take care of y'all like a real man does for his family. I don't want you taking the bus anymore. You deserve the best and I want to be the man to give it to you. I love you Kweeta."

"I love you too Bushwick," Kweeta replied, her eyes were now pouring tears.

"Awww," the crowd chimed in.

Bushwick opened the box revealing a 3ct Cubic Zirconia solitaire set in sterling silver, dipped in white gold.

"Kweeta, Shantika, Jackson will you marry me?"

"Yes!" she squealed.

"Bushwick slid the rock on her finger and the couple shared a kiss. The patrons of the restaurant cheered them on with applause and congratulations.

"Y'all heard that? My queen said yes! It's time to turn up! Cheddar biscuits for everybody!"

The waiter arrived with their appetizers and two glasses of champagne.

"The champagne is on the house. Compliments of the manager for your engagement, he announced.

"That's so sweet," said Kweeta.

"Good lookin' out bruh," Bushwick added.

"Would you like a full bottle in lieu of the occasion?" the waiter asked.

"Is it free?" Bushwick asked under his breath.

"No sir, only the first glass," the waiter replied.

"Naw, we good. Just bring a coke and two glasses of ice."

"Very well sir."

Once the waiter was gone Bushwick discreetly pulled a pint of Hennessey from his inside jacket pocket.

"I got us covered," he announced, giving Kweeta a sly wink.

"You always do boo!" she giggled. "Bushwick, you have made me the happiest woman in Watts. This ring is beautiful," she grinned, admiring her rock.

"Nothing but the best for my baby. Now you be careful with that. I still have six more payments on QVC before it's officially yours."

Meanwhile back at the house

Who the hell is this? Bernisha thought as she peeked out the window.

A Caucasian man had rang the doorbell several times and knocked on the door. After not getting a response he stepped off of the porch then looked back at the house as though he were checking for the correct address before looking at a notepad in his hand.

Ain't no way I'm letting his ass up in here. I know this has something to do with Bushwick. I wonder what type of trouble he's in. I don't know what my daughter sees in him.

Bernisha sent Kweeta a text as soon as he left.

It's a white man snooping around. He knocked on the door but I didn't let him in. Just wanted to give y'all the heads up.

Hmm, I wonder what that's all about, Kweeta thought, looking down at her phone. Whatever it was it would have to wait. She wasn't going to let anything ruin her evening.

Chapter 2 - Strange Encounter

After devouring a huge breakfast of hash browns scrambled cheese eggs, maple sausage links and grits Kweeta poured herself a cup of coffee and curled up on the sofa. This was her day off and she had to admit that it felt good having the house to herself. Bugatti was at school and Bushwick was starting his first day at Holla Back. She smiled when she looked down and admired her ring. She couldn't believe that she was really engaged. She and Bushwick had been through so much the past few years, but he had proven himself worthy of being her king.

No sooner than she snuggled under her favorite fleece throw and tuned into Judge Judy the doorbell rang. She wasn't expecting anyone. Friends and family usually called first. Not to mention it was only 9:30 in the morning.

"Who the hell could that be?" she mumbled, making her way to the front room to peek out of a crack in the blinds. She looked out just in time to see a Caucasian man headed down the walkway before hopping into an older model Honda Civic.

"What the hell? This must be the same guy mama was talking about from yesterday."

Now she was really confused. Was this dude with the narcs? She hoped Bushwick wasn't lying about not being in any trouble. As far as she knew she didn't owe anyone money, well no one who should be showing up at her door.

Since when did bill collectors make house calls?

Once he pulled off she opened the door and peeked out. She noticed that he'd left a card tucked in the security gate. The name on it read Michael Shepard, Private Investigator.

"Who the hell is watching us?" she asked herself, looking up and down her block for any suspicious parked cars before slamming the door shut. She had to admit that the fact that this dude kept showing up at her house made her a bit paranoid.

Her first instinct was to call Bushwick but she didn't want to bother him at work. After tossing the card on the coffee table she curled up on the sofa to resume watching her morning lineup. It wasn't long before her curiosity got the best of her. Each time she tried to focus on the television her mind drifted back to the card.

"To hell with it. I'm calling this damn number. Ain't nobody looking for me."

"Hello."

"Yeah…. Uhmm... may I speak to a Mr. Michael Shepard?"

"This is he, who may I ask is calling?"

"That's not important," Kweeta swiftly responded. "You left a card in my door. I'm curious why."

"I'm trying to locate a Kweeta Jackson," the man replied.

Kweeta's heart sped up. Her mind raced to figure out any reason she would be in trouble.

True enough, she had bounced a few checks around town, but that was over a year ago. Is it possible they could be on to her?

"Why are you looking for her?"

"Is this Miss Jackson?" the man asked.

"Yes it is," she replied hesitantly.

"I'm not too far from your home. May I come back so we can talk?"

Kweeta immediately became defensive. "You don't need to come back to my house. Anything you have to say to me you can say it over the phone," she snapped.

"Very well, can you confirm your date of birth?"

"What? Hell no! I'm not giving out any personal information to a stranger. Just tell me what you want."

"Is your father's name Hershel Jackson?"

"Yes it is. How did you know that?"

Kweeta's father had passed a few years ago. And even when he was alive it wasn't like they had the best relationship. She could count on one hand how many times they spent time together after he left her mother. He was known for always having some type of shady business dealings. Hopefully this wasn't the result of one of his scams gone wrong.

"Your father had a sister named Ola Jackson. She is the person that hired me. She was terminally ill for several years. She passed away a few days ago. I was instructed upon her passing to find her only niece. She has named you as the person she wishes to leave her inheritance to."

Kweeta sat shocked and dumbfounded. She had heard her daddy speak of a half-sister named Ola but he said they weren't tight. This seemed to be the trend within that family. But why would she choose her? If memory served her correctly she heard her father say Aintee Ola had two daughters.

"There must be some kind of mix-up. I didn't even know this woman. And how do I know you aren't bullshitting me?"

"With all due respect ma'am I was hired to do a job, nothing more, nothing less. If you are in fact Mrs. Jackson's niece you will need to be present for the reading of the will. If you have a pen I will give you the address to the attorney's office. The reading will be this Friday at 9:00 am. Bring your picture ID and a copy of your birth certificate."

Once Kweeta ended her conversation with the investigator she Googled him to see if he was really who he said he was. Sure enough she found several of his social media accounts including his profile on LinkedIn. Maybe this guy was telling the truth. She wanted to call her mother and sister but she figured she would keep the news to herself until she talked to Bushwick. Especially since there could possibly be some money involved. She knew if she told her mother and sister, they would be the first ones with their hand out.

Later that day

"Sounds like a set up to me. I mean why would she include me in her will when I haven't even met her?" Kweeta asked. "Plus she has two kids."

"People with loot do that type of stuff all the time. The kids don't turn out to be shit so they pass their fortunes on to complete strangers," Bushwick replied. "In your case she's still giving it to family."

"You might be right bae. Whatever the case may be we gon' check it out on Friday."

"Damn right! My baby might be in for a come up! We gots to be careful though. Imma come strapped just in case it's some shady shit on the horizon," Bushwick stated. "So you told anybody yet?"

"Nope, I wanna see how it plays out. If it's truly on the up and up. I wanna keep it on the low. You know folks can't wait to start begging if they think you got something coming."

The "folks" she was talking about was mainly her mother and sister.

Bushwick couldn't have been happier about Kweeta's news. True enough it might be bogus but at least it would keep her mind occupied so she wouldn't be too concerned about his new gig. When she asked him how his day went at work he grazed over the details. He was starting to second guess his decision to sign with Holla Back but he didn't want to say anything till he at least gave it a few days.

Once Friday rolled around the couple was up bright and early. Kweeta had already investigated and found out that the address was indeed an attorney's office.

Bushwick parked and left the engine running.

"Alright I'm going up in here but you know the drill," Kweeta announced. "If you see me running up out of there open the car door for me and be ready to peel out."

"Fa sho! And if they try to hem you up, shoot me a text and I'm rolling in with my finger on the trigger," he replied as he patted the steel piece in his waistband.

"I love how you always have my back," Kweeta purred before giving him a quick kiss. "Wish me luck."

Once Kweeta was inside the building she presented her credentials to the receptionist who directed her to a plush board room where several of Aintee Ola's family members were seated, none of which she knew. There were two women who appeared to be in their early fifties. These had to be her daughters. There was an older black man. If she had to guess she would say he was around seventy years old. None of them seemed too thrilled to see her.

No sooner than she stepped into the room the mumbling started. The other relatives couldn't understand who this strange woman was or why she was invited.

Kweeta took a seat at the far end of the table. "How y'all doing?"

No one responded. Instead one of Ola's daughters peered at her over her glasses.

"Who are you?" she asked smugly.

"I'm Aintee Ola's niece, Kweeta. Nice to meet y'all too," she replied rolling her eyes. She could already tell that they wanted to start some shit but she wasn't having it.

"Funny she never mentioned you," One of the old biddies replied sarcastically.

"I ain't never heard of you hoes either and yet we are here," Kweeta spat. If these old bitches wanted to try her she had time today.

The ladies gasped and clutched fake pearls.

"No wonder she never brought you up," One of the sister's said.

"My word! Not an ounce of class," the other one replied looking Kweeta up and down.

Kweeta jumped from her seat. "So wassup? You old bitches want a piece of me?"

She pulled her phone from her purse.

Before either could respond the older man spoke up.

"Now let's settle down ladies. There's no need for violence. I'm sure Ola wouldn't want us fighting.

Kweeta directed her attention towards him. "And you are?"

"Quincy," he said extending his hand. "I was Ola's butler."

Butler? Damn! Aintee must have been living large. "Nice to meet you Quincy. I'm her niece Kweeta."

"Nice to meet you Kweeta. This here is Phyliss and Wanda." He introduced the sisters against their wishes.

Neither bothered to acknowledge her. Kweeta took her seat, pulled out her phone and sent Bushwick a text. *Stay on standby, these bitches up in here wanna try me.*

Locked and loaded, he replied.

"I just don't understand why she's here. It's not like she ever came around," Phyliss said under her breath.

"We could say the same for you," Quincy coughed. "Don't let them bother you. It's obvious that you were invited. That means that you have as much right to be here as anyone else."

Kweeta couldn't help but giggle at the shade ole dude was throwing. She didn't need him stating the obvious but he was right. She decided she wasn't going to let these miserable bats knock her off her square.

No sooner that the words passed from his lips the attorney entered the room.

"Good morning everyone. My name is Justin BeeCroft. I am Mrs. Wilkin's attorney. I'm sure you all know why you are here. Mrs.

Wilkin's wished to distribute her belongings to her two daughters, Phyliss and Wanda, her butler Mr. Hawthorne and her niece Ms. Kweeta Jackson."

"Yeah, yeah we know….. cut the small talk and get on with the reading," Wanda stated impatiently.

Quincy rolled his eyes at the outburst.

"With all due respect I have to follow protocol," Mr BeeCroft replied. "If you have somewhere else you need to be I can gladly send you a notice with the portion you will receive in the mail."

He paused and raised an eyebrow at her.

Kweeta and Quincy snickered at the comeback.

Wanda was pissed but she wasn't going anywhere. She was too nosey. She was damned if she would leave without finding out what everyone else got.

"That won't be necessary," she replied drily. This bastard had some nerve trying to get flip with her. *Asshole, I should report him to the bar association. Whatever, as long as I get my piece of the loot. I'm the oldest so my cut should be the largest.*

"Very well. Shall we continue?"

"Yes, please go on," Phyliss replied, giving her sister the side eye.

Mr. BeeCroft slid a manila folder from his desk drawer. He pulled out a document and pushed his YSL glasses back on his nose.

"Let's start with her estates. The deceased has stated that the property at 3642 Willow street valued at $400,000 shall be shared equally among her daughters Phyliss and Wanda Wilkins. In the event that the property is sold, all funds shall be split down the middle. The vacation homes in Hawaii and Venice Beach shall be put up for sale. Mrs. Wilkins has asked that the proceeds go to the research for funding for pancreatic cancer."

"That's some bullshit! Are you sure it doesn't say that I'm supposed to get one of the houses?" Wanda griped.

"Mrs. Wilkins please let me continue. When the reading is complete I will be happy to answer any questions."

"Hush Wanda," Phyliss scolded.

The look on her face said that she wasn't pleased with the decision either but there was still her belongings, jewels, furs, designer bags and last but not least the money. Mama most likely didn't give them the houses because of the upkeep. She would most certainly make up for it with the rest of her assets.

"Next we have Mr. Hawthorne."

Quincy straightened up in his seat. He was nowhere near the greedy savage her daughters were. Over the twenty plus years that he'd worked for Ola and her husband he'd developed a friendship with them. Once Mr. Wilkins passed on, his role extended from just a butler to more of a care giver. He was one of the few people that she trusted. He wasn't surprised that she included him in her will considering she used to tell everyone he was like family.

Seeing as her daughters were more concerned with what she was leaving behind than actually spending quality time with their mother in her last days, this didn't sit well with her.

"Mrs. Wilkins wishes to leave you her jewels valued at 1.6 million dollars." Quincy almost fell from his seat.

Damn! Aintee was loaded! Kweeta thought. "Gone head Quincy!"

She laughed and patted him on the back as the sisters sat stoned faced.

"I am so grateful. I was not expecting that," he stated humbly as the tears fell from his eyes

"There's more," the attorney continued. "Mrs. Wilkins has also given you a cash gift of one million dollars."

"Thank you Jesus." Quincy lifted his hands to the sky.

"Won't he do it!" Kweeta shouted.

Wanda and Phyliss rolled their eyes in disgust. Wanda was two minutes from making a scene but she didn't want to be kicked out. She decided to play it cool and wait for the big announcement of the money she and Phyliss would be getting. Their mother was generous but she knew the bulk of her wealth would go to her children.

"All clothing including Mrs. Wilkin's furs and designer purse collection will be auctioned off with the proceeds going to the shelter for battered women."

"This is ridiculous!" Wanda spat.

"To Mrs. Wilkins daughters she leaves her complete book collection along with all of her houseplants."

Phyliss and Wanda looked at each other in confusion. There had to be some mistake. Wanda leapt from her seat.

"I don't want any fucking houseplants!"

Up until now Phyliss had maintained her composure, but even she had her limits. "Please sir, there must be some mistake."

"Damn right it's a mistake, Wanda fumed."

Quincy and Kweeta held in their laughter.

"Ms. Wilkins, one more outburst from you and I will have security remove you," the attorney stated. He was beginning to lose patience.

He then set his focus on Phyliss. "I assure you ma'am, this is what your mother requested. As I told your sister, everyone will be receiving a copy of the will. Now if I could please finish."

The sisters sat stewing. Their only hope was the fact that he hadn't finished yet.

"Finally, to her niece Ms. Kweeta Jackson she leaves her entire financial portfolio including cash, stocks, bonds, and CDs. Totaling in the amount of 156 million dollars."

Kweeta instantly became lightheaded. This couldn't be real.

"Hot damn! You done hit the jackpot," Quincy yelled.

Both Phyllis and Wanda stood to their feet.

"I know you a damn lie Phyliss screamed," now dropping her sweet composure.

"That's right! You tell em sis! I don't know what kind of scam this little bitch pulled but you got us all the way fucked up if you think you getting my mama's money!"

Wanda stood over Kweeta screaming to the top of her lungs, snapping her out of her trance.

Kweeta jumped in Wanda's face. "This ain't what you want old bitch!"

Mr. BeeCroft had about all he could take. "That's it, I'm going to have to ask everyone here to leave. I will be contacting each of you separately to go over the details of what you have received."

He then made a phone call out to the lobby and security promptly removed a screaming Wanda from the room.

"This ain't over! You ain't seen the last of me bitch! I will see yo' ass in court!"

Meanwhile, Phyllis sank back into her seat with tears rolling down her cheeks. "I can't believe that's all mama left us."

"I'm actually a millionaire. I can't believe it," Kweeta beamed.

"Believe it sweetheart, Quincy stated happily. He was thrilled that anyone besides Ola's sorry ass daughters had gotten the money. Karma was truly a bitch.

"You're not a millionaire yet. Like my sister said, we shall finish this in the courtroom," Phyliss yelled as the security gently took her by the arm and led her out the room. "Take your hands off me! This is harassment! I'm suing this law firm!"

Mr. BeeCroft shook his head before turning his attention back to Kweeta. "Congratulations Ms. Jackson." He smiled and shook her hand.

Kweeta's heart raced with pure adrenaline. However the excitement didn't stop her from taking the sister's words to heart. If it were one rule that she lived by, it was not to count your chickens before they hatched. Everything inside of her was exploding with excitement, yet she was almost afraid to show it outwardly for fear it could be taken away.

"Can they really take me to court to take the money away?"

"They can try but they would be wasting their time and money. Mrs. Wilkins has had her will set in place for years. Long before she fell ill," Mr BeeCroft assured her.

This put her mind a bit at ease bit she still didn't put anything past those sisters.

Lucky for Kweeta Mr. BeeCroft was right. The sisters' attempt at challenging the will in court failed miserably.

Chapter 3 – Loyalty Over Everything

"They straight clowning my nigga. That shit was all good when I signed on the dotted line. Now they trying to change up my image and everything," Bushwick ranted to his friend.

It had only been a few days but he could already see that Holla Back was not the label for him. When they scouted him out they hyped up how much promo and air time he would get. However, when he asked about when he would get to start laying down tracks, he constantly got the run around. He tried to chalk it up to the fact that his manager Duke Panty Dropper was busy and he had other people to manage besides him. However his gut instinct and canny ability to read people told him that this cat was full of shit.

Nonetheless, he at least wanted to give it a fair shot. To make matters worse he had asked Kweeta to marry him and now he wasn't sure if he would be able to provide for her and Bugatti the way he had hoped if this gig didn't work out. True enough Kweeta had come into some loot but that didn't help his situation. He was a man first and foremost and he wasn't about to have his woman taking care of him.

"Man that's foul as fuck! You know you gotta be careful with these labels. You should have had a lawyer look over your contract," Sedrick replied.

"Where the hell was I supposed to get some loot for a lawyer fool?"

True enough he had the money now because of Kweeta but when he signed a few days ago, it was on a wing and a prayer. He could hire one now, but he wanted to do this on his own. He wanted to be successful without Kweeta's help. His pride wouldn't allow him to have it any other way.

"My bad. Well look at it this way, you at least have that signing bonus."

Bushwick shook his head and sighed at his friend's remark.

"Wait? So you haven't received your advance yet?" Sedrick asked. "When are you supposed to get it?"

"That nigga be talking out the side of his neck every time I bring it up. He claims I'm supposed to be getting it tomorrow, we'll see."

"When does the contract say you supposed to get paid?"

"That's just it. The cash advance was a verbal agreement, they promised to tear me off something extra when I started," Bushwick responded, now realizing how crazy the notion sounded.

"Sounds like they playing you my nigga."

"These fools gon' fuck around and catch some heat if they don't cash a nigga out!" Bushwick ranted.

"Aye you know if the shit ain't adding up you still got a day to dip on they ass," Sedrick replied. "I know how the law works."

"Man what you talkin' bout?"

"Yo, I done watched enough Judge Joe Brown to know that you have three days to cancel a contract. They get to talking crazy tear that shit up."

"You bullshittin' me?"

"I'm serious. Nigga did you even bother to read the fine print?"

Bushwick took off his snapback and rubbed his head as he replayed the day he got signed. Normally he had an attention for detail, especially for something as important as his future. However, the big wigs at Holla Back had his mind so gone off the Yak and three blunts they had in rotation, along with the strippers they had pawing at him. Duke Panty Dropper even promised him his own Benz with the ladies included once his track blew up.

"I ain't gon lie. They had a nigga head spinning. I didn't look at the shit as closely as I should have," he replied with regret in his voice.

"That's how they get you my nigga! Gas yo' head up with all them hoes on yo' dick. They ain't selling shit, but a damn illusion. I thought you knew the game better than that my man."

"I do! They caught me slipping but imma be locked and loaded on they ass tomorrow."

Once Bushwick got home and reread over his contract he realized that Sedrick was right. He still had a day to legally get out of it. If they weren't playing on his terms he was calling it quits.

The next day

"Now calm down Bushwick, we are trying to sell records," Gloria Get Money, his publicist announced.

This broad was talking like a damn fool. One thing Bushwick promised himself was that he wasn't going to let the industry change him. Her request was ridiculous and he was putting his foot down.

"I don't give a fuck what you trying to sell. I ain't wearing no damn patch over my eye!"

"Come on man don't act like that," Duke chimed in. We need to thug up your image. Fetty ain't got but one eye and that shit worked for him. That patch will help up yo' street cred."

"Exactly, and I've even taken the liberty of typing up a story for you to tell the press as to what happened to your eye. We're going to say you lost it in a turf war," said Gloria as she placed a manila folder in front of him.

"Get that shit away from me!" Bushwick snapped.

"Aye man I suggest you calm down. All Gloria is doing is trying to help you," Duke warned.

"Man y'all ain't trying to help me. Y'all trying to have a nigga looking straight like a fool."

"How tall are you my man? 5'1, 5'2? Let's face it, there ain't too many opportunities out there for lil' dudes like you. Kevin Hart and Katt Williams are far and few between. I suggest you act a little bit more grateful and get with the program."

"I tell you what, fuck you and this contract," Bushwick spat.

Duke threw his hands up in the air. "Nigga you ain't said nothing but a word. We can step in my office and end this shit right here and now."

"Let's do it!" Bushwick replied boldly.

"Come on guys, it doesn't have to come to this," Gloria pleaded. Bushwick, think about what you are about to do. This is your career we're talking about."

"Nah, stay out of this Gloria," Duke spewed. "He want out, imma let him out."

With that he yanked open his desk drawer and pulled out Bushwick's contract. He grabbed a red marker and put a big red X on the page with the signatures.

"You try to give these hood ass niggas a shot at stardom and they don't even know how to handle business," Duke grumbled. "Soon as I find this addendum to the contract you can sign on the dotted line in our business will be finished."

"Fine by me," Bushwick said.

He sat quietly as Duke shuffled through the papers in his file cabinet. Despite the front he was putting on, deep down he was disappointed. Just when he thought the cards had been dealt in his favor, shit turned foul like it always did.

"Found it." Duke glanced over the addendum before placing it on the desk in front of Bushwick and handing him a pen.

Just as Bushwick was about to sign Duke placed his hand on the paper. "Once you do this there's no turning back."

Bushwick stared him dead in the eyes. "Move your hand."

Duke obliged and he signed.

The ride home for Bushwick was a bit somber. Just when he thought he'd gotten his chance at success he was back at square one.

The most frustrating part was the fact that he'd already asked Kweeta to marry him. Now here he stood once again without a job. He wasn't sure how she was going to take the news. He suspected that like the queen she was, she would be in his corner. That still didn't take away from him feeling like he had failed her. Once he parked the car he sat in the driveway for several minutes before making his way inside.

"Hey bae how was work?" Kweeta asked with excitement in her voice.

Bushwick's heart sank. Without him saying a word Kweeta immediately knew something was wrong.

"Hey bae," he replied softly.

"Wassup? Why you looking so down?"

Bushwick kicked off his shoes and threw his keys on the counter. He let out a heavy sigh and plopped down on the sofa "I quit my job today."

"Aww baby I'm sorry to hear that. You feel like talking about it?" She asked, taking a seat next to him.

"Man, they was trying to play me for a sucka. Come to find out the signing bonus was only $500. Plus they wanted me to do all kind of whack shit like wear patches on my eye and shit."

"Damn really? I'm not surprised. These so-called producers are shady as hell."

"Tell me about it," Bushwick griped. "The whole contract was fucked up. I swear I can't win for losing."

"Stop it right now. Don't go getting down on yourself. It's not your fault they wasn't handling business like they should. You'll find another job just like you found that one."

"Thanks bae. I know you just trying to cheer me up but I still feel like a piece of shit right now. It's not like an opportunity like that walks into a niggas lap every day. Hell, I can't even take care my fiancée and my baby."

Kweeta slid onto Bushwick's lap and gently turned his face towards her. Listen to me. What God has in store for you will be for you. Can't no man take it away. It's no need for you to feel like less of a man. You have always taken care of me and Bugatti. I know you will get a job and hold us down like you always do. But until then I got your back. We in this together."

The words she spoke melted his heart. It felt good as hell to have a down ass woman in his corner.

"Damn, what did I do to deserve you? I love you," he said softly before planting a kiss on her forehead.

"I love you too Bushwick."

The next day

"So how is his little rapping gig going?" Bernisha asked sarcastically.

For a second Kweeta toyed with lying to her. She hated to even tell her what happened. She took a swig of her caramel Macchiato before responding.

"He quit his job mama."

"I knew it!" That nigga couldn't keep that job for a week. Kweeta when you gon' drop his sorry ass?" Her face grimaced at the thought of this nigga laid up with her baby reaping all the benefits of her inheritance and wasn't bringing shit to the table.

Kweeta rolled her eyes. "I'm not leaving him mama. Bushwick has been good to me. And he's always taking care of me and Bugatti. He's just having a hard time right now. He feels bad enough already so don't you say anything to him," she warned.

"I ain't gon' say shit to him. I'm saying it to you. You need to stop slumming. That lil' nigga too damn old to be talking about a damn rap career anyway. I hate to see a man laid up with his woman taking care of him."

"You must've forgotten I'm taking care of you too." Kweeta spat. Her mama was working her damn nerves being so judgmental when she was the first one with her hand out as soon as she found out about the money.

"Don't get salty with me cause your man ain't shit. You ain't too old to learn a thing or two. And for the record I was taking care of my damn self while yo' ass was still slinging tacos."

If she don't shut her ass up she will be slinging tacos her damn self, Kweeta thought.

"Fine, don't listen to me. Yo ass gon' end up like Mary J Blige. Is that what you want? To wind up paying his ass alimony? I hope you at east have enough damn sense to get a prenup."

"Whatever mama. Just stay out of it I know what I'm doing"

Chapter 4 – Moving On Up

"It's beautiful Bushwick," Kweeta declared as she approached the front door of the splendid 6,750 square foot home in the heart of Beverly Hills.

"It's a beast. You sure we need a house this big?" Bushwick marveled.

"Boy please, now that we have this loot. I plan on having some more kids when we get married.

It had always been a dream of hers to live in the 90210 area code. The fact that she was about to make it a reality gave her goosebumps.

"In that case we need to hurry up and get up in here so we can get started," he joked and slapped her on the butt.

"May I help you?" the fortysomething year old Caucasian woman peered over her glasses at Kweeta and Bushwick.

Judging by appearance alone there was no reason they should have been stepping into a home in Beverly Hills. Surely they had to wander in accidentally.

"Hi, yes, I wanted to take a tour."

The woman cleared her throat. "A tour?"

"Yes, a tour," Bushwick clarified.

Kweeta instantly became annoyed because she knew what was up. What part of tour did this woman not understand?

"My apologies, but we aren't able to fit anyone in unless they have an appointment."

Here we go with the bullshit.

"So how do I get an appointment?" Kweeta asked.

Before the woman could answer an Asian, flamboyant gay male popped around the corner.

"Who do we have here?"

"I was just telling these kind people that they needed to have an appointment to take a tour."

Colin shot her a side eye.

"Nonsense! I can show you guys around right now."

The woman's face turned beet red.

"Thanks G," Bushwick stated. "We would really appreciate it."

"No problem, how soon were you guys looking to move?"

"If I find something I like, right away," Kweeta replied.

"Well I'm sure you will love this place. The owner just put it on the market so you are only one of five people who have had the privilege of taking a look at it."

"Let's do this!" Bushwick asserted.

"The home has six bedrooms and nine baths. Marble and limestone floors, The main level has exquisite dual great rooms a formal dining room, salon, and executive office."

"Wait, did you say salon?" Kweeta squealed.

"Yaaaas honey!" Colin replied with a snap of his finger.

"Now here to your right you have a lavish guest suite, and an enormous chef's kitchen with a breakfast room. In the event that you don't want to use one of these gorgeous staircases, there is elevator access to all three floors. The master suite has a fireplace, dual bathrooms, walk-in closets, and a private terrace. On the lower level you have a game room with wet bar, movie theater, temperature-controlled wine cellar, and a home gym."

Bushwick and Kweeta looked on in amazement at the vastness of the property. When they stepped outside they were met with a spectacular panoramic view of the city, manicured landscaping, covered seating areas an outdoor kitchen, and infinity pool.

It didn't take long for Kweeta to realize that this was the house of her dreams. She nudged Bushwick and whispered in his ear. "I think this is the one."

"Are you sure? We've only looked at a few places."

"Yes but it's something about this place. I can just see myself waking up here every morning."

"Alright Colin what kind of numbers are we talking?" Bushwick asked.

"The seller is asking 18,988 million."

Bushwick damn near choked on his own saliva. At the moment he had a cool $1.65 in his bank account. And he hoped Netflix didn't come out today and cause him to be over drawn. Lemme shut my ass up and let my baby handle this one.

"We want to make an offer!" Kweeta blurted out.

Colin was absolutely giddy. He clapped his hands together. "Marvelous! I just need to get some information from you and I will have the paperwork drawn up by in the morning."

"Thank you so much," Kweeta replied graciously.

She took one final look at the double spiral staircases and the breathtaking view. Once she was done giving Colin everything he needed they headed out. Kweeta was sure to give the woman who answered the door a grin and a wink on the way out.

The only glitch that Kweeta would run into was the fact that she had less than stellar credit. However, since she offered to pay for the house outright, it squashed all of that. Never in Kweeta's wildest dreams did she think her first home would be a mansion. The days of slinging dirty mop water and listening to customers complain was over. It was time to see how the other half lived.

Chapter 5 – Drip To Hard

"I don't know bae, I just don't feel right taking this."

Bushwick admired the Rolex Milgauss Kweeta had just bought for him. She'd already purchased him an entire new wardrobe, a Mercedes E class Sedan, and courtside tickets for the entire season of the Lakers games.

"Boy bye!" Kweeta waived her hand at him.

"I'm serious, you done bought me so much stuff already."

"And imma keep buying you stuff anytime the mood hits me. Ain't nothing wrong with buying my man a few gifts is it?"

"I mean, a nigga ain't complaining," he chuckled. "But I just feel weird not being able to buy you the same type of stuff in return, he continued on a more serious note.

Kweeta walked over to him and took a seat on his lap.

"Baby, please listen to me. I'm not worried about what you can buy me. You have always taken care of me and I love you for it."

Bushwick's heart melted when she said those words. He slid his arms around her, his head laid comfortably on her full bosom.

"That makes me feel real good to hear you say that. I know my little weed money ain't gon' cover much, but I still want to contribute."

"Bushwick. will you stop talking crazy? There's no need for you to do that now that we have money."

She was right. They didn't actually need the money. The point was, Bushwick still needed to feel like he was contributing in some sort away. Only time would tell how this would play out.

****

Chapter 6 - Pleased To Meet You

"What kind of name is Bugatti?"

"What kind of name is Bianca?" Bugatti replied, rolling her eyes. "You gotta problem with it?"

She realized that they were new to the neighborhood and she would have to make new friends, however she brought her hood attitude with her. Her mama had already warned her that they would be encountering people who might think that they were better than them, she told her no matter what, people were all the same no matter where they came from. And the character of a person mattered more than what they had. Because her mother had taught her how to handle herself in any environment she was well equipped and just as fast with witty comebacks as people were to throw sly comments. She was truly her mother's child.

"No I don't have a problem with it, dang I was just asking," Bianca replied nervously.

It was obvious that the new girl who'd moved in a few houses down was from the hood. She was a bit rough around the edges but she seemed cool enough.

"Well stop worrying about my name and bring your bike out so we can ride," Bugatti replied.

Bugatti balanced herself on her candy apple red shwinn with chrome hardware and a white basket on the front. She studied her potential new friend as she popped bubbles and twirled one of her box braids around her finger. She wasn't yet sold on Bianca. She seemed like she was stuck up but she might be cool.

"I told you I need to ask my mom."

"Who calls their mama mom?" Bugatti teased, scrunching up her face. She'd never heard this from any of her friends in the hood.

"People who speak proper English," Bianca responded rolling her eyes. "I'll be back."

Before she could turn to walk away her mother called her.

"Bianca!"

"Here I come!" She yelled back.

"Yes mom?" she asked as she made her way into the foyer of her elegant 5,000 sq-foot home.

"Who's your friend?"

"Huh? Oh that's Bugatti. She wants to know if I can bring my bike outside and ride with her."

"Hell no!" Austin yelled from the dining room after hearing his daughter's request.

"Mom…" Bianca looked at her mother with pleading eyes.

"Not yet honey. I need to meet her parents."

"You don't need to meet anyone," Austin hissed as he entered the room. "The answer is no. I'm not about to let our daughter hang out with some little hood rat."

"Austin please…" Zan cut him off in the middle of his rant. "How can you say that about a child? Besides, we don't know anything about those people. We don't have that many black kids on the block, it's good for Bianca to make new friends."

Bianca went to wash her hands and make herself a snack while her parents bickered.

Austin and Alexandria were a professional African American couple. The pair had met and college and married shortly after. They grew their wealth by selling real-estate in affluent neighborhoods such as the one they lived in. Having been long removed from the ghetto, Austin refused to entertain anything or anyone that reminded him of how poor he grew up.

"I know enough about them to know I don't want Bianca anywhere near that house. What kind of people name their child Bugatti? And you should have seen them when they moved in, blasting that ghetto music all loud. It was so many niggas running in and out of that house it looked like a damn plantation."

Zan rolled her eyes at her husband's excuse. If it were coming from anyone else she might have considered their opinion valid. However, she knew all too well that he could be a snob at times. Not giving some people a second glance if he thought they had some affiliation with the hood. As if the ghetto didn't raise both of them.

"I'm serious. Have you caught a glimpse of the couple that lives there?" He continued on. "The man looks like he just escaped prison and the woman looks like an extra for Set It Off. She looks just like one of those what do you call them?" he asked snapping his finger as he attempted to recollect his hood vernacular. "Trap queens."

Bianca busted out laughing from the kitchen. Zan even had to crack a grin at his corny ass.

"Ok I've heard enough, tomorrow I'm going to meet them and make my own judgement."

****

Chapter 7 – Rise And Grind

"I'm on my shit this morning. Time to stack this paper," Bushwick said to himself as he stepped out of the shower, lit a blunt and took a long drag.

Kweeta had offered to get up and make him breakfast but he had no time. There was more pressing business at hand. Since his contract fell through at Holla Back he was determined to make a name for himself on his own. With the help of social media and his keen business savvy, he was bound for success one way or the other.

After getting dressed he untied his durag and sprayed some oil sheen on his hair. Kweeta had redid his cornrows the night before. He slipped on a fresh pair of Jordan's and the Rolie on his wrist.

"Dressed for success," he announced as he admired his reflection in the mirror.

He grabbed a case of his CDs and checked his blunt stash. He had rolled twenty of them and planned on moving them at the high school a few blocks over. If he didn't know anything else, he knew rich suburban kids loved that good Kush from the hood. All he needed to do was hook a few of them up. Once word got out he was bound to make a killing. However, the first order of business was to solicit his music to his black neighbor a few doors down. He was certain that there were also white people on their block that listened to rap also but he had to case the area and get to know them better before he made his move.

He could have easily walked to the house but he wanted to show off his new whip. He hopped in and drove three doors down.

"Who the hell is this?" Austin grumbled as he looked out the window. The most excruciating noise he had ever heard was blaring from a pair of speakers out of the car that it just parked in front of his home. A few seconds later a miniature man emerged from the vehicle.

"Why is he coming here?"

Bushwick promptly rang the doorbell.

"May I help you?" Austin yelled through the door. He was not about to open it up for this thug.

"Yo, it's your neighbor."

"You've got to be kidding me." Austin flung the door open and looked him up and down. "State your business," he said with a stern voice.

"Hey man how you doing? I'm your neighbor from a few doors down. You can call me Bushwick."

Austin shook his head. He couldn't believe what he was seeing or hearing. It was obvious the neighborhood had gone to shit. "So you really drove three doors over?"

Bushwick held his stomach in laughter. Oh yeah about that, I wasn't going to do it but the whip was looking clean. I had to show him off. Know what I mean bruh?"

"No, I don't know what you mean. And I'm not your "bruh." Like I said state your business."

The ignorance is unbelievable. He's a perfect example of why my people can't get ahead.

Damn, what's up with this corny ass nigga? Bushwick thought.

"Sorry to disturb you man. I just wanted to come and introduce myself and see if you would be interested in some good music,"

Bushwick asked as he pulled one of his mixtapes out of his backpack.

"Surely you don't mean that garbage that you were listening to when you pulled up?" Austin chuckled.

Oh I see this nigga got jokes.

"You can just say you're not interested fam, you ain't got to call my art garbage."

Sensing that he'd hurt the strangers feelings, Austin had to catch himself. *I guess that was a bit rude.*

"I apologize Mr. Bushwick. No I would not like to buy any of your music now if you'll please excuse me I have work I need to get back to."

"Mr. Bushwick? What the fuck? All right man." He threw his hands in the air and walked off the porch.

"Well that didn't go as planned. The nigga had a whole stick up his ass. Fuck it. I'm not gon' let that shit sidetrack me."

Bushwick jumped back in his whip and headed to the high school a few blocks over.

"Watch me plug walk over here and make this loot. I know these little suburban ass kids like that good shit."

He parked across from the school until he noticed several groups of kids walking down the street. He then grabbed several blunts from his middle console and headed out after them.

"Yo' I got that good shit from the hood, what's up?" He asked, quickly flashing his product.

The first group of kids laughed and kept walking. He caught the attention of the second group.

"How much you charging?" A white boy that appeared to be around the age of sixteen asked.

"For you? $10 a blunt and there's more where this came from." Bushwick stated proudly

"I'll take one," another kid spoke up. He closely resembled the comedian Carrot Top with his bright red hair and orange freckles. He reached in his pocket and grab the loot. Just as they were about to make the transaction an unmarked police car swooped up to the curb and turned on a siren.

"Shit!" The kids yelled and dispersed

"Fuck!" Bushwick quickly turned on his heels and attempted to race back to his car.

"Freeze! Raise your hands in the air," the officer yelled.

Bushwick stopped in his tracks and raised his hands. This day just kept going from bad to worse.

"In jail? For what Kweeta asked hysterically.

"Baby please just calm down and listen. I need you to get me out of here."

"Tell me what you are in jail for Bushwick." Her voice shook with tears.

"Nothing serious. I just got caught with a few blunts."

"I'm getting dressed now. I gotta call my mama to watch Bugatti and then I'll be there."

"Thanks baby. Aye, don't tell your mama what happened."

"She's going to ask me where I'm going that I can't take Bugatti with me. What do you want me to do? Lie to her?" There was a time Kweeta would have lied without her giving it a second thought but now she'd gotten fed up with Bushwick acting so immature.

"You know she won't let me live this shit down if she finds out I'm back in here again. Just do me this favor baby please," Bushwick pleaded

Kweeta rolled her eyes. "I'll be there shortly,"

Kweeta arrived to the jail and Bushwick was released with a $5,000 bond. Aside from his car being impounded, he had court next week and was advised that he couldn't leave the state.

"Listen Kweeta I know you mad at me but I had to do what I needed to do."

Do you realize how stupid you sound? You didn't just get caught with a few blunts as you tried to put it. You got caught attempting to distribute to a minor," she fumed. She couldn't believe she was going through this shit with his ass once again.

"Just hear me out. I needed money to take care of my family. Yeah I know you got your money and stuntin' and all. But how you think that makes me feel as a man? You already know how hard it is for me to get a job. I had to hustle the only way I know how. I ain't gon' lie, trying to sell to the kiddos was probably a bad idea. But I know these rich fuckers love that good shit. I just need a good connection on this side of town."

"Do you hear yourself? Are you trying to go back to jail?"

"What kind of simple ass question is that. Obviously you ain't listen to shit I'm saying."

Kweeta softened her voice. The last thing she wanted to do was kick her man while he was down.

"Bushwick I already told you I don't give a damn about you contributing to the household right now. I understand you're a man and you want to take care of your family and I'm not trying to take that away from you. That's exactly why I told you I would invest in whatever business you wanted to start. A car wash, a barber shop whatever."

Bushwick was appalled.

"I don't need you to buy a business for me. That ain't doing nothing but just reinforcing what I'm already saying. I can't do shit for myself."

Bushwick realized that Kweeta was trying to help but it only made him feel worse. His insecurities mounted when he thought about the type of circles Kweeta would be able to move in. Even though they both came from nothing she at least had money. With her he did also. But on his own he had nothing and he didn't like not being able to measure up. To the average fuck boy this would've been his dream. However, to a man like Bushwick who was used to taking care of his family, it gave them a feeling of less than. It would only be a matter of time before his insecurities totally consumed him. This caused problems in their relationship. No matter how much Kweeta built him up emotionally, no matter how much she try to encourage him, it still felt like something was being handed to him and he didn't like it one bit.

****

Chapter 8 – I Gotta Leave You Alone

"Why does he gotta be so damn difficult?" Kweeta fussed as she headed to the gym to blow off some steam.

Lord knows she loved Bushwick with all her heart but she was beginning to wonder if he was truly her soulmate. She was doing everything she could think of to encourage him and to let him know that she was in his corner but he just kept messing up. The crazy part is, she didn't knock the nigga for trying to get his hustle on. But the point was, he didn't have to. It's not like they were still in Watts barely scraping by. They had enough money to fuel any dream he could think of and he chose to sling blunts like he was broke.

The thought of her mother possibly being right is one of the things that hurt her the most. This was the very reason she chose not to tell her or her sister what went down. Both of them would jump at the chance to bash him and judge him and she didn't feel like dealing with the drama. For the first time in the four years they had been together, she actually thought about leaving him. She was trying her best to make it work but he needed to get his shit together.

****

Chapter 9 – No New Friends

"Leave me alone," Bianca stammered nervously.

"Shut your little bougie ass up!" the bully yelled in her face.

Bianca blinked away the tears.

The group of older girls encircled her and began pushing her around. One of them snatched her backpack.

"Give it back, Bianca said, her voice shaking.

"Or what?" One of the bullies sneered. What yo' little scary ass gon' do?"

The truth was, she didn't know what she was going to do. This was the second time this month the group of bullies had cornered her as she was leaving the girls locker room after gym. The first time they had taken her lunch money and threatened to beat her ass if she told anyone. She dreaded to think what they had in store for her this time around.

"Leave her alone!" A voice from behind them boomed.

They turned to see Bugatti standing before them holding a metal baseball bat.

"Who the fuck are you," Reese, the biggest of the bullies hissed."

Bugatti squared up with the juvenile wanna be thug and looked her dead in the eyes.

"The bitch who's gon' bust yo' head to the white meat if you don't leave my friend alone."

The other girl's eyes grew wide. They had never witnessed anyone standing up to Reese. Bianca's heart thumped in her chest. Reese stood with her chest out and snarled at Bugatti.

"Looks like we have a certified bad ass," she laughed.

"I'm not afraid of you," Bugatti asserted, never once flinching.

She didn't know who these little tricks were but they damn sure didn't scare her. She was from the hood and used to taking up for herself. And she damn sure wasn't about to be punked by some lame ass girls from Beverly Hills.

Reese was lowkey shook but tried to play it off in front of her girls. Truth be told, she didn't know how to take Bugatti. She'd never seen her before. But she sensed that she was serious about her threat.

"Whatever, give her the little stupid bag back," Reese instructed.

For the first time her squad saw the fear in her eyes. They didn't know who the new girl was, but if she was bold enough to stand up to Reese they figured they better not try her.

"Take your bag little hoe!" the second bully croaked as she threw the bag in Bianca's direction.

"You better watch your ass around here." Reese tried to get one final bluff in with Bugatti but she wasn't moved.

"We can go right now. Why wait?"

Reese's pulse quickened. She opened and closed her sweaty palm trying her best to look hard in front of her crew. The truth was, none of them had actually been in a fight. They just never ran up on the right one.

Just then the bell rang.

The squad dispersed.

Bianca was finally able to breathe. "How did you do that?"

Bugatti tossed the bat to the floor. "I didn't do anything. You just gotta stop letting those tricks run you," she replied as she took off walking in the direction of her class.

"But…. they outnumbered me."

"They wasn't gon' do nothing." Bugatti's street sense kicked in where Bianca's sheltered suburban upbringing failed her.

"How could you tell?"

"I don't know…. You just know. They looked scared. Anyway I gotta get to class."

"Me too, thank you. Hey, you wanna ask can we ride to school together?"

Bugatti shrugged her shoulders. "That's cool."

Bianca's face lit up. "Ok! I'll ask my mom as soon as I get home."

****

Chapter 10 – Welcome To The Neighborhood

"You're being ridiculous. If anything you should be happy that someone was there to help our daughter," Zan stated.

Austin rolled his eyes. "Please, if she really wanted to help she should have went and got an adult instead of teaching our child that violence is the way to handle things."

This was an odd statement coming from Austin seeing as he'd been known to fly off the handle with Zan on several occasions.

Bianca normally wasn't a disrespectful child but her daddy was being totally unreasonable.

"Daddy, if she wasn't there those girls would have jumped me. She scared them away."

"Lucky for the both of you that her little vigilante plan worked. You could have gotten seriously hurt. We still don't know if they are going to try and retaliate. I'm not raising my daughter to brawl like she's some sort of savage."

"And I'm not raising our daughter to be a punk. I'm glad Bugatti was there to stand up against those little brats," Zan said. "You know what? I don't know why I bother."

"I don't know either…." Austin turned the volume back up on the tv and proceeded to ignore his wife and daughter's defense campaign for Bugatti.

Zan placed her hand on her daughters shoulder.

"Go put on your shoes, we're going to pay your friend a visit."

"Yay!"

Bianca leaped into action.

Once they were at Bugatti's house Bianca eagerly rang the doorbell.

"I don't know who it is but they ain't gettin' up in here," Bushwick announced after looking out the peephole.

"Who is it?" Kweeta asked walking up behind him.

"Some nerdy lookin' chick and a kid. Probably Jehovah Witness."

Kweeta looked out to see a pretty African American woman in her mid thirties and a little girl.

"That looks like the little girl Bugatti was playing with the other day."

She cracked open the door.

"May I help you?"

"Hello, I'm sorry to disturb you. I'm your neighbor from a few doors over. My name is Alexandria but all my friends call me Zan. This is my daughter Bianca."

"Nice to meet you Zan." Kweeta shook the woman's hand. "I'm Kweeta and this is my fiancé Bushwick. And hello to you Bianca." She also acknowledged the child.

"How y'all doing?" Bushwick added, still not sure what the visit was about.

"Is Bugatti home?" Bianca blurted out.

"Bianca don't be rude honey. We just stopped by to thank your daughter for helping Bianca at school yesterday."

Kweeta's brows twisted in confusion.

"Please come in."

Bushwick gave her a "*what are you doing*" glance.

"So what exactly did she help her with?" Kweeta asked as she led them to the spacious living area.

Zan couldn't help but notice how gaudy the home was decorated. The fur rugs, ceiling to floor bling along with the African inspired art that looked like it was bought from a corner swap meet, didn't allow her eyes a place to rest without being assaulted. With that being said, it was a perfect representation of the home's owner who donned a tailbone length honey blonde lace front, stripper heels, faux Versace print leggings, and a hot pink tube top.

"Thank you, we won't be long. My daughter was being bullied at school yesterday and your daughter stood up to them and protected Bianca."

"Really?" Kweeta asked.

By now Bugatti had made her way downstairs.

"Bugatti come say hi to your friend and her mother," Kweeta instructed.

"Hi," she said waiving at the both of them.

"Miss Zan says you helped Bianca get away from some bullies. I'm very proud of you," Kweeta beamed with pride.

"So am I," Zan added.

"Thank you," Bugatti stated shyly, not used to the attention on her.

"No, thank you!" Zan gushed. "I don't know what would have happened if you weren't there."

"They would have kept messing with me," Bianca acknowledged before walking over to Bugatti and giving her a hug. "Thank you."

"Aww, isn't that sweet?" Kweeta added.

"That's my baby!" Bushwick said. "She don't take shit off nobody!"

Kweeta shot him a sideways glance. "Anyway, I'm glad to see Bugatti has made a friend. The school needs to do something about those bad ass kids."

"It's my understanding that this isn't the first time Bianca has had a run in with these girls. I plan on paying the principle a visit first thing Monday morning."

"Can me and Bugatti ride to school together?" Bianca asked.

Zan's voice stammered at being put on the spot. "We'll have to talk it over with your daddy sweetie. And we would have to make sure Bugatti's parents are ok with it."

"Please! Can we ride together?" Bugatti pleaded.

"We'll see," Kweeta replied. She wanted to get to know her neighbors a bit more before she committed to letting her child being driven around by them. She was sure Zan felt the same way.

"Me and Bushwick need to talk as well. I'll let you know."

"No worries, I'll talk to Austin as soon as I get back home."

"Austin? Is that your husband?" Bushwick asked.

"Yes, have you two met?"

"Yeah, I met his lame…." He was about to finish but Kweeta nudged him in his side. "Yeah we met."

"Great! Looks like the girls aren't the only two that have made friends. We won't take up any more of your time. It was very nice meeting the both of you."

"Nice meeting you as well," Kweeta responded as she walked them to the door.

No sooner than they left Bushwick couldn't wait to express his displeasure in the idea of Bugatti riding to school with Bianca.

"I don't want Bugatti riding to school with that girl."

"Why not? The kids like each other. And her mother seems nice enough. I mean I know we should meet her father."

Before she could finish Bushwick cut her off.

"I already met her punk ass daddy."

Kweeta raised an eyebrow. "Oh, so that's what that little episode was about. What's up with him?"

"Ain't shit up with him except he's corny as hell."

"When did you guys meet?"

When we first moved in. I went to go introduce myself and try to sell him one of my CDs."

Kweeta laughed to herself. "Let me guess, he didn't want to buy it?"

"Of course not. You know it's some lame-ass negroes living in Beverly Hills. That nigga wouldn't know good music if it slapped him in the face."

"That's not a reason to keep Bugatti away from Bianca."

"It's not just that. He was trying to act all high and mighty. Like we weren't good enough to live in the neighborhood. You know I ain't about to kiss nobody's ass."

"Is that what he said?"

"Not exactly but it don't take a rocket scientist to know when you not wanted. I'll be damned if my baby is going to feel that way if he's driving."

"That's understandable, and if we find out that's how they are Bugatti doesn't have to ride with her. But her mom seems cool with it and the girls like each other. And who's to say we can't be the ones driving them?"

Bushwick immediately became annoyed. "See that's the shit I'm talking about. A nigga can't get no type of respect up in his own home. Oh, I forgot this is your house."

By now he had pissed off Kweeta. "Don't go there just because you in your feelings about that mixtape. You know perfectly well this is both of our home. This is about the girls, not you. You need to put your ego aside and let Bugatti have a friend."

"I've said my piece. Like I said, I see my words don't mean shit."

"Not when you talking crazy they don't."

Kweeta noticed the change in Bushwick's demeanor. He was grumpier than usual and seemed to complain a lot more. He never snapped at her this way in the past. The money should have made their life easier but in contrast, it seemed to be more of a curse.

****

Chapter 11 – People In Glass Houses

"Thanks girl, you know how much I appreciate this," Cherokee acknowledged.

"It's cool but I can't keep giving you money," Zan noted. "I hate keeping things from my husband."

If this bitch only knew.

"I totally understand, I will repay you back as soon as I can. I'm trying to get my shit together. It's just hard out here."

"Cherokee I don't understand why you don't go back to school. You're a smart beautiful girl with everything going for you." Zan tried to motivate her.

Cherokee let out a heavy sigh. "If only it were that easy. The truth is I hate school. But my ass has to do something and fast. They trying to foreclose on the house," she sulked.

"Damn Cherokee, I didn't realize it was that bad. Can you go to your family?"

Cherokee let out a hearty laugh. "Chile please! That's a joke right? My family ain't gon' do shit for me. It's not like they would if they could anyway."

"Well, we're gonna have to do something," Zan said with concern in her voice. "We can't let you get put out."

"Don't worry about me," Cherokee replied before taking a sip of her lemonade. "I got a few sugar daddies lined up."

Who was she kidding? She didn't have shit.

Cherokee's claim to fame was her short stint on basketball wives. Once her character was written off the show she was back to square one. An LA native, and Instathot beauty, in her mind she should've blown up by now. She did manage to nab a baller and achieve a nice settlement in the divorce along with the house she was currently living in. However, poor budgeting skills, lavish vacations, and extravagant shopping sprees quickly depleted her funds. She was currently on the prowl for a new sponsor. In the meanwhile she was scraping by anyway she could.

Of course she could've gotten a job like everyone else. But that wouldn't have funded the lifestyle that she was so accustomed to. The part about her not being able to go to her family was true. None of them could provide the type of money that Cherokee wanted. $100 here or $50 there would do nothing for her. That was lunch money on any given day. She was the epitome of house poor. Meaning yes, she had the house but she couldn't afford much of anything else. As of now the 32-year-old had been able to skate by on her looks alone. However, now she felt the clock was running out. As it stood, the taxes in Beverly Hills proved to be more than she could handle, but they would have to drag her out kicking and screaming before she gave up her house.

"Hey, don't forget that Kweeta is coming with us to the cooking class."

"How can I forget. Since when did this become a threesome?" Cherokee grumbled.

"Since her daughter helped Bianca. Her and I have been keeping in touch. She's actually really nice. You should give her a chance."

"I guess… you know I like to keep my circle small. I have a reputation to uphold. We can't be letting no pigeons up in with us."

Zan smiled but didn't respond. This chick was the last person to be calling someone a bird.

****

Chapter 12 – If You Can't Stand The Heat

"Hello everyone and welcome to the Madame Larue gourmet cooking class. My name is Skylar McNeil and I will be your instructor today. Before we get started does anyone have any questions?"

One of the students raised her hand. "Yes, I was wondering how long you have been a chef?"

"I have been a chef for over 25 years. I've worked in some of the most world renowned restaurants across the globe. It's my pleasure to bring some of my most favorite recipes to you here today," She replied with a smile. "Anyone else have questions?"

The class was silent.

"Very well then let's get started. Today we will be making roasted duck in orange sauce, sautéed broccolini, For an appetizer we will have a delicate tuna tartare. And for dessert a decadent Crème brûlée."

"That sounds delicious, Zan squealed." The rest of the class gave similar sentiments.

Kweeta however, was less than thrilled.

"Yuck, who the hell want a damn roasted duck? Can a bitch at least get a Cornish hen and some wild rice? Some shrimp Alfredo? Something."

Mrs. McNeil noticed the distressed look on Kweeta's face.

"Is everything Ok Miss Jackson?"

"Yeah, I was just hoping to be making something a little more soulful."

Cherokee rolled her eyes, "Oh God here we go. I told you not to bring her ghetto behind," she said under her breath while nudging Zan.

"I assure you Miss Jackson the dishes will be flavorful and delicious."

Once class was underway Kweeta took notice of the selection of seasonings that was given to them.

"Y'all ain't got no Lawry's up in here?"

The entire class erupted in laughter.

"They won't have Lawry's in here Kweeta. This is a gourmet cooking class," Zan noted. She had to admit that Kweeta was a bit embarrassing.

"And? Rich people don't like seasoning on their food? That's why I'm glad I came prepared."

With that she opened her purse and pulled out a Ziploc bag containing Adobo seasoning, Lawry's seasoning salt, lemon pepper seasoning, and garlic salt.

Cherokee was mortified. "You've got to be kidding me. Oh my God this is the last time I go anywhere with her."

Meanwhile Zan found Kweeta's actions hilarious.

"I'm sorry Ms. Jackson but outside spices are not permitted in the class."

"for real? Alright well I'll put it up after I season my stuff. Y'all can do yours how you want but I need some flavor.

Kweeta then proceeded to give her meat and veggies a generous sprinkle. When it was time to put the duck in the oven Kweeta opted for cutting it up and deep frying hers. At this point the instructor had totally given up on trying to get her to follow directions.

"Tender as mother's love!" Kweeta called out as she pulled off a piece of the fried duck.

By now the class was hysterical.

"I actually wanna try that," one of the class members said.

"It smells delicious," another one called out.

Zan and Cherokee couldn't believe what they were seeing. A crowd began to form around Kweeta's area as she passed out samples of her duck along with the broccolini she'd smothered in cheese sauce.

"Come on Zan! Get you a piece before it's gone."

"Hang on, let me grab a plate."

"What are you doing?" Cherokee griped. "Don't encourage her."

"What? It looks good. I kinda wanna taste it."

Skylar threw her hands in the air and left the room.

Kweeta noticed Cherokee sitting by herself trying to act brand new and addressed her.

"Churches ain't got shit on Kweeta's fried duck. Gon' and try it." With that she slid a paper towel in front of her with a piece of meat.

Cherokee reluctantly took a bite. She had to admit it was pretty tasty. The skin was seasoned and crispy while the center was tender and moist. Kweeta and Zan waited for her response.

"It's good…."

"I knew it!" Kweeta cheered.

"Let me get another piece."

Chapter 13 – We In This Bitch

"Look at the white shoes…." Bushwick sang as he danced around like Jerome from Martin, showing off his new Gucci golf shoes.

"I see you boo!" Kweeta cheered him on.

"Imma kill these niggas on the golf course."

"Bae, you ain't never played golf before."

"They ass ain't either. Imma win by default for inviting they ass," he joked.

"I been meaning to ask you about that."

Bushwick could sense the uneasiness in her tone. "Wassup?"

"Who all did you invite? You know this is a classy country club. I know they said we can bring a few guests but you know how your boys are."

"Don't worry. I done already warned them not to embarrass us in front of all these white folk. They promised to be on their best behavior."

"I hope so. I don't know why you invited them."

"Because they my boys. You said I could invite who I wanted."

"True, but you also know them niggas are known for showing their ass." Kweeta shook her head in disgust. This was their first time visiting the Grand Luxe country club and she wanted to make a good impression. Once they arrived they made their way to the lush golf course. A spread of decadent hors d'oeuvres awaited them.

"Damn it's lit as fuck in here!" Bushwick blurted out.

No sooner than the words escaped his lips his phone vibrated in his pocket. It was his boy Sedrick.

"Yeah man where y'all at?"

"We outside. They won't let us in."

"I told y'all fools to text me first. I'm on the way."

"They outside," he told Kweeta.

"I'll go with you."

It didn't take long before Kweeta and her crew were noticed. There was already a bit of skepticism about letting her join in the first place. However enough money can get you whatever you want.

"Damn bruh! Y'all living your best life!" Sed belted out.

"Lower your voice," Kweeta chastised. She glanced around to see if anyone noticed the outburst.

"Bae. Why you trippin'? They just being themselves, let them have some fun." Bushwick was embarrassed himself, but it was because Kweeta was acting all boughetto in front of his friends.

Once the game was underway the day went from bad to worse. Bushwick's crew yelled at each other up and down the golf course. They flirted with the waitresses. One of them even had the nerve to bring a speaker on to one of the golf carts bumping Bushwick's mixtape while rolling down the course.

"Aye y'all check out my man's new CD! He spittin' that fire. Available now on Soundcloud!"

Bushwick doubled over in laughter. That's my boy! That nigga always looking out."

"Eleven!" Wayne yelled out as he scooped up his loot.

"I'm done, this nigga cheating,"

"I'm with you dog, this nigga done won three times. Them dice gotta be loaded," Bushwick added.

"Excuse me sir, I am going to have to ask you to please turn the music down and leave the golf course," a staff member announced.

"Why? Is it because we black?" Ken belted out.

"You know it is," Bushwick wailed. "They didn't want us in here from the jump."

By now a crowd was beginning to form and security had been called.

"Y'all always trying to keep the black man down," Sedrick yelled.

"I assure you this has nothing to do with race sir. You gentlemen are being disruptive and we have to ask you to leave."

Man, fuck that. That's why we need to learn to be comfortable in our own spaces I knew this shit was gon' be foul before we even got up in here," Bushwick grumbled.

Kweeta returned from the bathroom and noticed the commotion in their section

"What the hell?"

She walked up to see Bushwick and his crew being escorted out.

"What's going on?"

"These bougie ass white folks hating on niggas!" Wayne belted out.

"I'm sorry Miss Jackson but I'm going to have to ask you and your party to leave. They were being very disruptive. And drugs are not allowed on the golf course."

"Drugs," Kweeta asked in confusion.

Bushwick waived his hand. "They just trippin' because Sed fired up a blunt. The shit is legal so I don't see what the problem is."

The onlookers were now growing in numbers. When it was all said and done not only was Kweeta and her party escorted from the club. Her membership had also been revoked. She was livid to say the least.

"I don't believe you Bushwick! How could you embarrassed me like this? I warned you before we left that you shouldn't have invited them. Why niggas gotta always act like they ain't used to shit?"

"Because they ain't! Duh! Anyway, I'm sorry I'm an embarrassment to you. Forgive me for not meeting up to your new standards."

"Boy shut the hell up. It ain't got nothing to do with new standards. It's about acting civilized when you go somewhere and not making a damn spectacle of yourself. They showed their natural black asses. I'm not going to let you or anyone else make me look bad."

"Make you look bad?" Why do you want the acceptance of these white people so bad?"

"Fuck you." Kweeta didn't make a habit of cussing at Bushwick but this nigga had lost his damn mind.

"Fuck me and I'm just telling the truth?" I've said it once and I'll say it again. That money done changed you. I don't know who you are anymore."

"Maybe it has changed me, but it's for the better. Forgive me for trying to better myself and surround myself with the finer things in life. Damn right, I changed. I've spent my entire life struggling. I'm still the same down ass chick from the hood. That part of me will never change. But at some point we all can stand to change something about ourselves. You my man so of course I want to take you along for the ride. The problem is, I can elevate you financially but you will have to elevate yourself mentally."

"Oh, so now you saying a nigga stupid?"

"I never said that. But the fact that everything I just said went right over your head makes me question it. I'm just saying, sometimes you have to let people go. You can't hang with the same people that you used to hang with and do the same things that you used to do if you expect to get ahead in life. Number one being your ignorant ass friends."

"You know what? You right, sometimes you do need to let people go. Imma start right here. This shit is over."

"What are you talking about," Kweeta asked, her voice beginning to shake.

"You heard me. It's over. I thought we were gon' be able to make it after you got the loot. But I see now I ain't good enough for you and your new way of life."

"I NEVER SAID THAT!"

"You ain't got to say it. Actions speak louder than words. And they damn sho screaming right about now. I'll pack my little shit I came here with and be out of your house in the next few days."

"Why are you trying to blow this up into something it doesn't need to be? Nobody said they wanted to break up. You just on some real fuck boy shit right about now. Trying to avoid the truth about your friends and refusing to take responsibility for your actions." Kweeta was hurt but she'd be damned if she was going to back down when she knew she was in the right.

"I'm done with it." Bushwick threw his hands in the air and walked away from her.

"So you're really going to throw us away behind this shit right here?"

Everything was happening so fast that Kweeta didn't have time to fully process it. The truth was, the country club incident was only the tip of the iceberg. The real issue was that Bushwick's insecurities had grown to epic proportions. It caused him to think irrationally. At this point there was nothing Kweeta or anyone else could do to change his mind. The pair slept in separate rooms for the first time in four years. Kweeta's heart was crushed. She cried herself to sleep that night. Bushwick kept his promise and was gone by the next morning.

****

Chapter 14 – She's Out Of My Life

"I just can't believe it's over," Bushwick sulked before slamming a shot of Patron.

"Man, I told yo' crazy ass to chill. That's a good woman you lost," Sedrick replied.

Bushwick had come to him to vent but little to his knowledge Sedrick was actually happy to hear things had gone south. He wasn't one to betray his boy on a normal basis but that loot had Kweeta lookin' real good.

"Nigga you think I don't know that? I knew that damn money was going to be the worst thing that ever happened to us," Bushwick reflected.

Look at this nigga not taking responsibility for shit, Sedrick thought.

"Damn right it was. And let's not forget you walked out on her. Kweeta was already a beautiful woman. Now she's got racks on top of it. What she need yo' little ass for? How much you wanna bet she's going to find her a nigga with some coin to match hers? Hell, I wouldn't be surprised if she even got herself somebody with some height on him."

Sedrick cut his eyes at Bushwick to see if his speech was successfully working on his ego.

"What the fuck! Who's side are you on?" Bushwick spat. I didn't come here to hear this shit."

"You need to hear it. A real friend ain't gon' sugar coat this shit. They gon' tell you the truth. You fucked up a good thing with Kweeta by letting your pride get in the way. You'll be lucky if she ever speaks to you again."

Bushwick lowered his head. Sedrick's word's stung like salt in an open wound. but everything he was saying was the truth. Now that Kweeta had money she was exposed to a different crowd. Men who were shitting on him looks and financial wise. He had never been this down on himself but he still held out hope that love would prevail.

****

Chapter 15 – I Can Love You Better

"This nigga done fucked up an I'm about to slide right in his spot."

Sedrick slid off his durag and ran his hand across his 360s. Kweeta had never been his type but her recent financial windfall made her look fine as hell in his eyes. Bushwick was his boy and he hated to do him dirty, but this nigga was acting like a straight clown.

Ain't no way his midget ass should have been complaining about shit. There are men that would kill to be in his shoes. To be a stay at home husband while their girl foots the bill for everything. It sounded lovely to him. If and when he got in, his plan was to knock her up as soon as possible to secure the bag,

"Bushwick's dumb ass let pride get in the way of getting his money. I'm 'bout to show Ms. Kweeta what it feels like to be loved on by a real man. Plus she needs a nigga with some height on him now that she has money. How the hell is she gon' look walking into events with a garden gnome escorting her? Shiiit, for as much money as that bitch has, she can wear the muthafuckin' pants and the strap on too."

It was true. Sed wasn't gay but he was willing to bend over, literally if it meant he no longer had to live the rest of his life in poverty.

Chapter 16 – Missing Him

Kweeta wept silently as the hot water ran down her back. It felt like her heart had been ripped from her chest. In the entire four years she and Bushwick had been together they had never been apart. Whoever said money can't buy happiness damn sure told the truth. It seemed like they hadn't been happy since she acquired that money. She stepped out the shower and begin drying off. Her focus soon turned to the ring on her finger. The tears once again began to fall. How ironic that she had all the money in the world to buy any piece of jewelry she wanted, yet the ring from Bushwick meant the most to her. The diamond may have been a replica but the love was real. The worst part about it all, she didn't feel like she had anyone she could talk to.

Sure she had a few girls. But truthfully she had to move on from most of them as well as some of her day ones that she thought would be there forever. She had friends that completely turned on her when they found out about her newly acquired wealth. It wasn't like her sister and her mama were any better. Bernisha never liked Bushwick from the jump so she would revel in the chance to talk trash. Same went for her sister, when in fact the way her relationship, or lack thereof, was setup, she had no room to judge anyone.

Once she was dressed she made herself a cup of coffee and sat out on the back patio to clear her head. As she admired the view she wondered what was the point of having all these beautiful things in life if she didn't have anyone to share it with. She made her way back inside, figuring she would veg out on the sofa for the rest of the day with Netflix and junk food.

It wasn't long before depression began to rear its ugly head.

"I got to get out of this damn house. It feels like the fucking walls are closing in on me."

Against her better judgement she called the only person who was kind of like a friend to her at the moment.

"Hello."

"Hey girl what are you up to?"

Zan immediately became concerned with the tone of Kweeta's voice.

"Hey, I'm not up to anything, are you okay it sounds like you've been crying."

"Actually no, I'm not. I need to get out of this house just to go have a drink and talk. I don't know, maybe I need to have a spa day."

"I'm down. I'm free all afternoon." Truth be told Austin had been working her nerves as well. A spa day sounded perfect.

"Okay, meet you in an hour at your house?"

"I'll be ready. Hey, do you mind if I invite Cherokee?"

"That's fine, the more the merrier."

Kweeta dragged herself back to the bathroom and applied her makeup before changing into a more appropriate outfit. She then pulled out her newest lace front. It was a 30 inch body wave beauty. After gluing it down she pulled it into a playful high ponytail and left a few tendrils hanging.

"Hey girl come on in. Cherokee should be here in five minutes. Can I offer you anything?"

"No thank you. I'm good."

When Kweeta stepped into the home the first thing she noticed was the stark difference in their taste of decor. Zan's style was much more classic and understated. This equated to boring for Kweeta. The same went for her personal style as well. From her simple chin length bob to her J.Crew boyfriend jeans and Banana Republic tshirt, topped off with a pair of Hermes ballet flats. Kweeta knew enough about designers to know that her outfit probably cost more than some people's entire wardrobe. However to her it was just so drab with no flare no excitement. *Oh well, to each his own.*

"So what's going on with you?" Zan asked.

Kweeta's throat began to tighten up at the mere thought of what she was about to say.

"Me and Bushwick broke up."

"Oh no sweetie. I'm so sorry to hear that."

"It's all good. It was for the best. Sometimes people just outgrow each other. Better to find out now instead of later on after wasting money on a wedding. Know what I mean?" Her mouth was saying one thing, but her cracking voice said another.

Zan walked over and gave her a hug.

"I hope you get back together but I don't live with you guys. Only you know what's best for you. Anyhoo, I found us this hot new spa on Rodeo Dr. After we're done with our treatments we can grab a bite and chit chat."

Kweeta didn't know whether she was coming or going. She was just happy to get out of the house.

The doorbell rang. It was Cherokee.

"What's up ladies?," she sang as she sashayed through the door.

"Hey girl," Zan replied

"How you doing?," Kweeta acknowledged her.

She'd met Cherokee once before at the cooking class. The encounter was so brief she couldn't decide whether she liked her or not. Although she did detect a stankness about her attitude. In contrast, Cherokee knew off the bat that she didn't care for Kweeta. however, for the sake of remaining cool with Zan she played along.

"I can't wait to get to this spa. I'm getting the full treatment, Cherokee gushed.

"You and me both, Zan added. "I can't remember the last time I've been pampered."

"It shows," Cherokee raised an eyebrow at Zan's chipped up fingernails.

Zan didn't bother giving her sarcasm any attention. Kweeta peeped the exchange but didn't say anything.

Once they stepped foot inside the spa the relaxing atmosphere immediately put Kweeta's nerves at ease. After the ladies chose their services they were led to dressing rooms where they disrobed and changed into plush terry cloth robes. While they waited for their spa attendants to arrive they relaxed while sipping on cucumber water. Kweeta opted for the deep tissue massage followed by a facial, manicure and pedicure. As the therapist worked on the knots in her shoulders, the stress of the past week melted away. She emerged feeling like a new woman.

"You ladies ready for a light lunch?" she asked.

"Count me in," Zan replied.

"I'm down, Cherokee added.

"Kweeta your skin is positively glowing," Zan complimented her.

"Thanks girl, it's that prickly pear massage oil. It did wonders for my skin.

"It sure did. And I'm loving the color you chose for your toes and nails."

Cherokee rolled her eyes. She'd gotten a manicure and a pedicure herself but no one seemed to notice.

"Yeah I got my toes and nails done too."

"Yours is nice also Cherokee," Zan added, never once mentioning that she'd gotten the same treatment herself.

This bitch can't stand for the attention to be on somebody else, Kweeta thought.

"It's so cute up in here! I love the way they have it decorated." Kweeta admired the plush silk tablecloths and purple tufted chairs.

Once again Cherokee tried to throw shade. "Girl is this your first time seeing this place? I'm a regular here."

Just as Kweeta was about to snap on her, Zan stepped up.

"And? So what it's her first time let her enjoy it."

Once they were seated and placed their drink order they proceeded with girl talk.

"I have to thank you ladies for getting me out of the house today." Zan said. We need to do this more often."

I don't know about us doing it all together. Kweeta thought, *I can't see myself hanging with this bitch again.* "Tell me about it, I've been stressed out as hell."

Zan took a sip of her mojito. "It's going to be okay girl. Just give it some time."

"I hope so. Right now I feel like crap. I broke up with my dude," she announced looking at a curious Cherokee.

"Oh, I know how that feels that's why I be like fuck catching feelings. Might as well use these niggas for what you can get out of them. They gon' end up breaking your heart anyway. So who's the side piece?"

"Cherokee!" Zan scolded. "Must you always be so damn rude?"

Cherokee shrugged her shoulders. "I'm just asking a question."

"She alright. I did just put it out there. For the record no. Bushwick has never cheated on me."

"Not that you know of," Cherokee smirked as she primped in a mirror compact.

Miserable hoes stay projecting shit. "No. Bushwick didn't cheat on me. He just got off house arrest and got himself in trouble again but he wasn't a hoe. He was just having a hard time getting a job. He got caught up in the streets. His mix tape wasn't doing well.

Amongst other things that caused a strain on the relationship. He's just down on his luck and my glow up made him feel insecure. I told my boo I would always be there to hold him down. But Bushwick is a true hustler at heart. He wasn't about to stand by and let his bae handle all the bills.

Zan and Cherokee's mouth fell open.

"Whoo chile, the ghetto!" Cherokee busted out in laughter.

"Whatever bitch, don't try to act like yo' shit don't stink." Kweeta had, had about enough of this hoe.

"Touché, I ain't gon' lie, I done fell for plenty of fuckboy's in my day. But at least they had their own coins. You messing with a grown ass man trying to sell mixtapes? Not to mention he's what 5'1? 5'2? And the nigga is a jailbird, I'm just saying, pick a struggle."

At this point she'd pissed off Zan as well. "You're totally out of line for that," she snapped. "Don't make me put all your business out in the street."

Despite Zan's laid back demeaner, she wasn't one to mince her words. The last thing Cherokee wanted was her to get wound up and blast the fact that she was about to lose her home, and not only was she borrowing money from her to catch up on bills, Zan had footed the bill for the spa day as well as the lunch they were currently eating.

Aww shit! I wonder what the tea is on this bitch, Kweeta thought. The fact that Cherokee backed down with the quickness meant Zan must have some real dirt on her ass.

Their attention was drawn to the sexy, chocolate, 6'4 business man that was walking towards their table.

"Who is this?" Kweeta asked.

"I don't know but he's wearing the hell out of that Versace suit," Cherokee replied. She straightened up in her seat and pouted her lips.

"He is handsome," Zan had to admit.

"He's coming over here," Cherokee announced. "Imma need y'all heffas to fall back."

"Hello? I have a husband," Zan reminded her.

"Don't nobody want him. Here, have some water to quench that thirst," Kweeta joked as she pushed her glass of water in front of Cherokee.

"Whatever, watch and learn how a true diva secures the bag," she countered as she adjusted her breast, making sure they were sitting high.

"Good afternoon ladies."

"Hello," Kweeta and Zan sang in unison.

"How you doing handsome? You can call me Cherokee," she purred.

"Nice to meet you Cherokee. I'm Basil."

"I'm Zan, nice to meet you."

He gave her a nod. "The pleasure is mine Zan.

"And who might you be gorgeous?" He asked, his dark eyes piercing into Kweeta.

"I'm Kweeta."

The immediate chemistry between the pair was evident by the longer than usual eye contact. Cherokee noticed the exchange and cleared her throat.

"So what can we do for you Basil?"

"I saw this beauty from across the room and had to get a closer look," he replied never taking his eyes off Kweeta.

Zan giggled at the shocked look on Cherokee's face.

"Thank you." Kweeta blushed at the compliment.

"You're quite welcome Kweeta. If you don't mind me asking, are you single?"

She paused a second before answering. The only guy she'd been with in the past four years was Bushwick. It was awkward interacting with another man in this manner. Zan nudged her under the table to snap her out of her trance.

"Yea… yes."

"Great, I would like to get to know you a little better if that's ok with you."

"I'm ok with that."

"If you pass me your phone I will add my number," he said with a seductive smile.

By now Cherokee was shook. *This dude must be fresh out of prison or have cataracts. How is he going to pass up filet mignon for a fucking patty melt?* She rolled her eyes in disgust.

As Kweeta passed Basil her phone their fingers gently brushed each other. After passing the phone back to her he instructed her to call him so that he could save her number.

"Got you locked in. I look forward to talking to you."

"Look at you bagging fine business men and we just got here!" Zan squealed as he walked away.

"I don't know why I took his number. I doubt if I talk to him," Kweeta replied. The truth was, the breakup was still fresh and she was still in love with Bushwick.

"Why not? I mean I know you have just gone through a break up but it can't hurt to have a nice conversation with a handsome man. Who knows, he may even get you out of the house. It will do you some good," Zan encouraged her.

The idea of going out with another man was a bit unsettling to Kweeta but after looking at his credentials she would at least consider it.

"It says here that he's a sports promoter for Nationwide Sports."

Zan's eye's widened. "That's only the top marketing company in the country!"

"I'm not impressed," Cherokee stated dryly. "How do we even know if that's his real occupation? That nigga could be a fraud in a suit."

"Stop being a hater Cherokee. You're just mad because he didn't give you a second look."

Kweeta was two seconds away from checking the shit out this trick but seeing as Zan's drink had kicked in, she handled it for her and saved her the breath. She decided right then and there that this bitch was a vibe killer and this would be the last time they would all hang together.

"Chile please! I'm the last bitch to be sweating a fake Bill Gates negro. I'm just saying, he seems like he's got an angle. I wouldn't be surprise if he's on the downlow. You know them type always looking for a female to be a beard for them."

****

Chapter 17 – Afternoon Tea

"Well I'm proud of you," Bernisha stated. "I thought you was never going to get rid of that little muthafucka. You don't know how many nights I prayed that you would come to your senses. I asked God to remove him from your life. And for a minute I thought he wasn't listening. But my God don't do me wrong."

"Won't he do it?" Laronica sang.

Kweeta shook her head at the performance these two were putting on, if it were anyone else she might be more apt to listen. But neither one of them had room to talk. It was sad to see that they were praying for her and Bushwick's downfall.

"Whew chile yes! I mean Bushwick was cool and all don't get me wrong. But you can do way better."

Kweeta looked at her sister sideways. "You can too. But I guess we aren't going to talk about Elroy chasing after anything in a skirt. Anyway, y'all ain't talking about shit. I still miss him."

Laronica sucked her teeth but she couldn't argue with the truth. "That's natural, you'll get over him soon enough though. The point is, you took a step in the right direction."

Bernisha nodded her head in agreement as she stuffed her face with her third slice of pizza.

"Hold that thought. Lemme go check on the girls."

Kweeta excused herself and made her way to the back door. Bugatti and Bianca were chilling on the patio eating pizza and having girl talk much like the grownups inside. She was about to ask them did they need anything when she overheard them talking.

"Boys are so stupid," Bugatti stated after sharing her story of how Theodore Dixon makes it a point to pull her hair when he sits behind her in class.

"Tell me about it. I hate boys too," the eleven year old agreed.

Kweeta smiled at the girls proclamation. She was about to stick her head out the door when Bianca continued.

"And I'm never getting married when I grow up, especially if he's like my dad."

Bugatti frowned. "Why do you say that?"

Kweeta stood frozen in her tracks.

"He can be really mean to my mom sometimes. When he thinks I can't hear them arguing he yells at her and calls her names."

Bianca's throat began to tighten as she fought back tears.

Bugatti's eyes widened. Despite her growing up in the hood with what mainstream society would call ghetto parents, this was new to her. On the contrary, her parents never yelled at each other, nor had she ever heard her daddy call her mama out of her name.

"For real? What does he say to her?"

"He calls her stupid and tells her that she is worthless. He calls her the b word sometimes too.

"Dang that's messed up."

Kweeta covered her mouth in shock.

"Why doesn't she leave him?" Bugatti asked.

"I don't know." Bianca looked down. She could no longer hold back the crocodile tear that was about to fall. Sometimes I wish she would. When it's really bad he shoves her around and tries to scare her."

"That no good son of a bitch," Kweeta said under her breath. She could hear footsteps approaching from behind.

"Girl where you at?" Laronica called out.

When she approached the doorway Kweeta put her finger to her lips to shush her. Laronica caught on that Kweeta was eavesdropping and joined in.

"That's crazy." Bugatti shook her head.

"I know. Sometimes I hate my daddy. He thinks he's cool but he's so corny. I wanted to get some box braids but he told my mom that I couldn't get them because he said the style looked too ethnic."

Bugatti didn't know what to say behind that. She was just a kid but she had enough sense to know Bianca's dad sounded foolish.

Laronica was just about to respond when Kweeta took her by the elbow and led her down the hall back to the room they were sitting. She didn't want the girls to know she overheard them.

"Did you hear that bullshit?" Laronica asked.

"Yeah I heard it. Her daddy as lame as fuck," Kweeta fumed.

"What y'all talkin' about Bernisha asked.

"That girl's daddy had the nerve to tell that baby she couldn't get braids because it would look too ethnic," Laronica replied.

"Where they do that at?" Bernisha questioned.

"Apparently out here in Beverly Hills. These bougie ass negros done forgot where they came from," Laronica added.

Kweeta couldn't argue with her on that point. She was still shook at the fact that Austin's punk ass was abusive towards Zan.

"Chile I never thought I would see the day when I would be agreeing with Bushwick but he's right, you need to stop Bugatti from hanging with that little girl." Bernisha said.

"Hell yeah I don't want that stuck-up shit rubbing off on my niece."

"It won't, Bugatti has a solid foundation. And I'm not going to fault the child because her daddy is an asshole. She didn't let on to the rest of the conversation she'd overheard. There was no need to share considering these two would have nothing but negative feedback.

"Anyway, back to what we were talking about. I ran into that guy I told y'all about."

"And…. When are y'all going out?" Laronica asked.

"Y'all don't get it. It's too soon. And like I said, I still have feelings for Bushwick," Kweeta replied sadly as she gazed down at her ring.

"Chile if you don't take that gumball machine ring off and go out with that man…" Bernisha fussed. "Ain't nobody say you gotta walk down the isle with him, but at least see what he's about."

"I agree with mama. Giiiirlll, this might be your Russell Wilson," Laronica added.

Bernisha nodded. "That's right think about how Ciara would have ended up if she kept wasting time with Past Tense and his harem.

Kweeta took their words to heart, As much as she hated to admitted it, Bushwick seemed like he wasn't ever going to get his shit together. Who knows, maybe she would go out with this guy.

Chapter 18 – Unsecure Bag

"So what does this bitch have on me?" Cherokee asked as she nibbled on a rice cake.

"Bitch, what you over there talking about?" Essence piped. Do you know niggas love Ayesha Curry?"

"I know, that's what I'm saying, why though? Is it because she got that good girl look? Shit, I can pull that off," she said as she glanced at herself in the mirror thinking that she should change her hair and lighten up on the makeup.

"That's part of it, aside from her being beautiful. You know niggas love that wholesome shit."

"Both of y'all hoes wrong," Chrissy added. You're forgetting Steph was with her since they were kids."

"Yeah that's got to be it because I know that bitch don't look better than me. I got to sit in the VIP section of the club where the Warriors were sitting the last time they played at home. I'll give it to her, she got that nigga sprung. Either that or his ass is gay, he wouldn't bite for shit."

Essence busted out laughing. "You sound dumb as hell. That's a married man. "You ever thought about he might just be faithful to his wife?"

"Girl bye!" Cherokee waived her hand. "All athletes got bitches on the side."

"True," Chrissy chimed in. "But the competition is tight. You know they got hoes in every area code."

"What we need to do is take our ass to Vegas during the summer league." Essence suggested. "Those boys are ripe for the picking."

"I'm down," Cherokee agreed.

After she and her girls gossiped and swapped stories of which ballers had "flewed" them out the past week, it was time for them to go.

"Ok well it's time for y'all hoes to go," Cherokee announced standing from her seat. "I got a dick appointment."

"Ok bitch. Why you didn't tell us you was working tonight?," Chrissy giggled.

"I'm telling y'all now. See y'all later."

After her girls left Cherokee hopped in the shower then slipped on a pair of sexy yoga pants and a crop top with no bra. Making sure her nipple bar piercings were on full display. She then spritzed on some Flower Bomb and ran a brush through her 24 inch lace front. Granted, she was joking while they were there. But the truth was, deep down she didn't know what the hell she was going to do. She didn't have any jobs lined up. And none of her usual tricks were biting. This money that she was getting today would help keep the utilities turned on. Just as she took a swig of her drink she heard a knock at her back door. She made her way to the door and peeped out the window before cracking it open.

"You're early," she said in a little sexy tone.

"The wife fell asleep early." Austin stated as he walked in the house.

"You hungry?"

"So what if I am? I know you didn't cook shit," Austin replied smugly.

"Shut the hell up. I've been taking gourmet cooking classes with your wife."

"Oh yeah how's it working out?" He asked as he took a seat on the plush suede sofa.

"It was fine. I mean it could've been better if she didn't invite that ghetto ass Kweeta to hang out with us."

"Yeah I don't know why she insists on making friends with that sewer rat."

"So what's your pleasure today daddy?"

Austin smiled while grabbing the growing bulge in his pants. "Daddy needs some lip action."

Cherokee was ready to oblige. She went to the bathroom and placed her hair up in a ponytail. Part of her felt bad for working this nigga and his wife for loot but fuck it, she had to do what she had to do. If he wanted his dick sucked then so be it. She marched back in the room ready to go to work. She slid down between his legs eager to please.

"Whatever you want daddy. You know I'm here to take care of you."

She unzipped his pants and pulled his manhood from his underwear and proceeded to stroke it to full hardness.

"Come on. I don't have that much time," Austin encouraged her as he nudged her head towards his erection.

Cherokee took the tip of his meat in her mouth and gently begin to suck. Austin relaxed back in the sofa. She then slid down his shaft taking him entirely into her mouth. He let out a loud groan as the tip of his dick tickled her tonsils. She slurped up and down till he was sopping wet. She then moved her head back to the tip and bobbed it up and down while using both hands in a twisting motion to jerk him.

"Don't forget the balls he grunted."

She gently begin fondling his balls before tracing her lips down his penis and gently taking them into her mouth. She sucked and slurped them down while continuing to jerk him. He guided her head back up to his dick and proceeded to hold it in place while he fucked her mouth. As the pleasure grew in intensity he thrusted away while she squirmed and gagged.

Austin couldn't hold out any longer. He removed himself from her mouth and pushed her back on the sofa. Her tits bounced freely as he yanked up her top. He let out a loud grunt as he unloaded himself on her breast.

"Damn that was pretty good," he panted as he collapsed on the sofa.

Cherokee wiped her mouth then walked over to the kitchen and rolled off a few paper towels to clean herself off.

"I'm glad you enjoyed yourself."

"All right well I guess I'll see you around in a few days."

Austin proceeded to zip his pants. As he headed towards the door Cherokee stopped him.

"Wait, what about what you said you were going to give me?"

Austin frowned. "I don't recall saying I was going to give you anything."

It was true. He didn't actually say he was giving her any money this time around. But she automatically assumed he would take care of her as he always did. The fact that she had to ask made her cringe.

"I normally don't have to ask. You usually just take care of me."

"Oh yeah, about that. It's about time you find yourself a new sugar daddy."

Cherokee threw her head back. "Say what? So what you're saying is you done with me?

After I been given you the bomb ass head that your wife can't provide. And this tight ass snatch that hasn't pushed out any babies?" She said with a smirk on her face. She was only partially joking.

Austin looked down his nose at her. "Don't flatter yourself. I've had better. I'm sorry but you have nothing coming."

Cherokee was livid. The nerve of this son of a bitch. "So why did you let me suck your dick if you knew you weren't going to give me anything?"

Austin shrugged his shoulders. Hey, I'm a prude but still a man. I'll take a free blow job anytime I can get it."

"You know what? Fuck you Austin! How about I tell Zan everything?"

Austin doubled over in laughter. "You won't do that because you're broke. If you're lucky I might buy you a few groceries so you don't have to eat Top Ramen next week."

Cherokee sucked her teeth. "I see why she calls you an asshole."

Austin smirked. "Is that what she calls me? Anyway, look I'm sorry if I hurt your feelings but you have me all wrong if you think you're getting any more money out of me. Like I said, I may toss you a few dollars for some groceries if you need it but other than that this is probably going to be the end of our little sessions."

With that he left. Cherokee stood dumbfounded. "Now where the hell am I going to get my bill money? Up until now Austin was a sure bet. However she'd made the ultimate hoe mistake. She'd gotten too comfortable and put all her eggs in one basket. Now she was truly fucked.

****

Chapter 19 – Girl Talk

"Damn girl, so what attracted you to his ass in the first place?" Kweeta asked as she listened to Zan's rant.

"He was on the basketball team in high school. He was super smart and fine on top of it. All the girls liked Austin."

"Wow, I would have never imagined," Kweeta said before realizing how rude she sounded. "Damn, did I say that out loud?"

"It's ok," Zan laughed. "I understand how you can say that. Especially since he hasn't exactly given off the best first impression. But like I was saying, Austin was my dream guy back in school. His drive and ambition is what got to me the most. He was determined to get us out of the hood and make something of himself."

"And how was he treating you back then?"

"Back then? He treated me like a queen."

"As he should have," Kweeta nodded as she sipped her Moscato.

"Even up until the first few years we were married. Everything was blissful. It wasn't until he closed on a huge deal and we moved to Beverly Hills. That's when everything changed," Zan reflected with sadness in her eyes.

"So basically the nigga started feeling himself."

"If only it were that simple. That's what I thought at first. But it's like the money changed him for the worse. He's lost touch of who he was."

"That still ain't no excuse for him talking to you the way he does. I'm not even around him that much but the few times I have been, he's condescending as fuck. Not to get in your business, I'm just saying."

Kweeta was trying her best not to go there for fear of overstepping her boundaries. But seeing as Zan opened the door by starting the conversation she figured she'd give her two cents. This was the nicest way she knew how to tell her girl that her man was an asshole.

"You're absolutely right. It has become a major issue in our relationship."

Zan shook her head. "I just don't know how we ended up here. I've been looking into a few marriage counselors. That is if I can get him to agree to it."

Kweeta noticed Zan's mood taking a dip and decided to change the subject.

"Anyway… I'm still trying to decide if I'm going out with Mr. Sport's Promoter."

"You should go! It would do you some good to get out of the house and have some fun."

"That's the same thing my mama and sister said. It's just too soon. I'm not ready to move on."

"You're looking at it the wrong way. Don't look at him as a future mate. Just someone to have some fun with."

"Maybe you're right."

When Zan left Kweeta called Basil and the date was set.

****

Chapter 20 – First Impressions

Come open the door.

K.

Kweeta responded to the text she'd gotten from Zan before taking a swig of her Hennyrita. Her doorknocker ear rings clanged against each other as she bounced down the stairs.

"Hey!" Zan squealed when she opened the door.

"Hey girl," come on in."

"So wassup? Why did you call me over here?"

"To talk me down from flaking on this dude."

"Don't you dare. You have been avoiding him for weeks. You can't bail out now. I mean you can but why would you? You said yourself that you need to get out of the house and have some fun. Why not do it with a handsome successful man?"

"You sound like my mama and my sister. Imma go, but a bitch nerves is on edge," Kweeta replied before finishing off her drink and pouring herself another and taking a huge gulp. "You want a drink?"

"Sure, I'll have one. You need to slow down though. You don't want to be drunk when he gets here."

"Please, I can handle my liquor. I just need to take the edge off."

"What are you drinking?" Zan asked as she suspiciously eyed the pitcher Kweeta was pouring from.

"Hennyrita, made with lime koolaid.

Kweeta filled a cognac glass half full of the green concoction and passed it to Zan.

What kind of section eight fuckery is this? Zan thought as she took the drink.

She realized that she was acting just as boujie as her husband but she hadn't drank anything remotely this weird since her college days, much less out of a cognac glass.

Oh well, it is what it is. She took a swig and almost gagged from the sweetness.

"Good ain't it?" Kweeta asked proudly.

"Actually it's not bad. It's just super sweet."

"It's an acquired taste. If it tastes too sweet that just means y'all need to step ya Kool-Aid game up at home."

Ole boujie asses, Kool-Aid probably sour as hell.

"Actually we don't drink Kool-Aid."

I knew it! "Damn girl. Y'all don't do shit to remind y'all of the hood huh? I ain't mad at you though."

"It's not that. We just try to live a healthy lifestyle. We don't want Bianca having that much sugar. Anyway, enough about me. Are you excited? What are you wearing tonight?"

"Yeah I'm excited. I'm nervous as hell. It just feels weird going out with another man."

"I totally understand. I don't know what I would do if I were single again."

"Hold that thought. Lemme throw on this fit real quick."

Kweeta disappeared to her bedroom and reemerged ten minutes later Fendi down to her toenails.

"What you think?" she asked as she spun around giving Zan the full view.

Zan was taken aback from the head to toe logos. Kweeta had the Fendi print leggings and cropped jacket, along with Fendi print over the knee boots with a matching logo chain belt and signature logo bag. Her iced out stiletto nails with the double F logo completed her look.

"Wow…"

"I know right? This outfit is fire! His ass ain't gon' know what hit him!"

Got that right…. Uhm, Kweeta, you mind if I make a suggestion?"

"Go head girl."

"Maybe you should tone it down a bit."

"Tone what down? My hair or my makeup?" Kweeta asked as she gazed in the mirror.

"Everything," Zan replied cautiously.

"Say what?" Kweeta snapped her neck around.

"Hear me out. I understand you are used to dressing a bit flashy, but didn't you say he was taking you to an upscale restaurant? Maybe try something a little classier."

No this heffa didn't. "You trying to say I ain't classy? What's more classy than Fendi?"

"No, I'm not saying that…." Zan backed down realizing she'd open a can of worms.

"So what are you saying then? I can't dress?"

"It's just that… well.. when you wear labels from head to toe it takes away from the style of the brand and it becomes tacky." She hated to put her girl on the spot but she needed to hear the truth.

Kweeta smacked her lips. *I know this no style having ass hoe did not just call me tacky.*

"Girl Bye! How you gon' tell me how to dress when you up in here looking like a soccer mom?"

"Uhmm, I am a soccer mom."

Zan didn't take kindly to the insult. Although her everyday attire was laid back. She could jump clean when the time permitted. And it would be done with class and elegance.

"My point exactly. Until you get some style of your own you need to fall back."

It was obvious that Zan's advice had hit a nerve with Kweeta.

"Listen Kweeta I wasn't trying to hurt your feelings. I was just trying to spare you the embarrassment of showing up at an establishment looking like a clown."

Shots fired! Ok it's time for Condoleezza Rice to get up out of here.

"Ok girl, I think it's time for you to go."

"I think it is too. And let's not forget you invited me over," Zan countered.

She normally wasn't this snippy but Kweeta's attitude prompted hers.

"Don't worry, you won't be getting another invitation," Kweeta snapped as she walked her to the door and slammed it behind her. "The nerve of her corny ass. Anyway, let me get my mind right."

Kweeta turned up the volume on her Bose sound system.

"Time to test out these boots!"

She paraded around the room as Mary J Blige, Family Affair blared through the overhead speakers. She looked in the mirror and kicked out her leg, practicing Mary's signature moves just in case they went dancing. After a few more sips Kweeta realized that she was tipsy and better slow it down.

"Lemme chill my crazy ass out before a bitch needs another shower."

Once Kweeta was done getting dressed it was time to be on her way. The alcohol managed to put her at ease, but she still didn't feel totally comfortable with going out with this dude. It was almost like she was giving in to the peer pressure. He offered to either pick her up or send a car for her. She chose neither seeing as she didn't want him to know where she lived. When she arrived at the restaurant she sent him a text.

Hey, I'm outside.

Great I'm on my way out.

When Basil saw Kweeta he couldn't believe his eyes. She was still the same beauty that he was attracted to from the first time he saw her. Yet today she looked like an extra for Love and Hip Hop. From the rap video outfit, garish makeup, and blinged out stiletto nails, she was dressed the total opposite of his semi formal attire. The gentlemanly side of him didn't give any indication that he was displeased with her style choice. Instead he moved in for a hug and greeted her.

"Hey beautiful. It's good to see you again."

"Hey, it's good to see you too."

They went in for a brief hug and Kweeta immediately took notice of his hard upper body in broad shoulders. The scent he wore was intoxicating.

"Our table is all set. I hope you like Italian food."

"I love Italian food."

Basil was pleased that he got it right.

"Score one for me. So how have you been?"

"I can't complain."

Kweeta realized that she was keeping her answers short and to the point but it had been forever since she'd been on a date with anyone besides Bushwick. It felt awkward to say the least.

"That's good to hear. I know you've been busy the past few times that I've called."

"You trying to throw shade?" Kweeta cocked her head at him sideways. He had her all the way fucked up if he thought he was going to dictate when she answered the phone.

"Excuse me?"

"I said are you trying to throw shade, I know a sly comment when I hear one."

Basil smiled. I assure you sweetheart I wasn't trying to "throw shade." I was just taking note that you seem to be a busy woman. You know you can let your guard down around me."

The truth was, he *was* trying to throw a slick comment out there but she caught onto it. He wouldn't let her know this though.

Kweeta relaxed back in her chair and took a sip of water.

"My bad. Yeah, I've been running a lot of errands lately."

"Really? So what do you like to do in your spare time Ms Kweeta?"

"I don't know, shop, get my nails done, I love a good scary movie."

"Scary movies huh? That's good to know. I'll keep that in mind for the next date. Or am I being too presumptuous?"

Presumptuous as hell. Kweeta gazed at her date as he spoke. She didn't know much about him on a personal level but from the outside looking in he was the entire package. He had everything that many women lusted after. He was handsome, successful, and charismatic. Not to mention he was dressed to the nines. His deep mahogany complexion showcased a killer smile and sexy deep set eyes. Yet, she wasn't attracted to him.

"We shall see. I'm also looking into opening a hair salon."

Basil raised his eyebrows. "Ahh, a businesswoman, I love it. Do you like doing hair or is this just something you are investing in?"

"I love doing hair. I always have."

Kweeta used one of her razor sharp talons to brush her bangs to the side as she spoke. "It will be a full service salon. Braids, sew ins, lashes, make up, you name it. I want to offer the works."

Basil took a sip of his wine before replying. "That sounds great. You should do well considering how much money women spend on those type of services."

"I'm hoping so. I just need to make sure I get a good location."

"Me personally, I prefer the natural beauty of a woman."

Here we go with the shits, Kweeta thought.

"So you one of those brothers that don't like women to wear weave or make up?"

"I don't mind a little make up if it's done correctly. Just enough to enhance her beauty. As far as the hair, no, I'm not fond of the horses mane."

Basil realize that these were direct jabs at Kweeta but she may as well know where he stood from the beginning if they were ever going to become an item. She would have to tone it down drastically.

By now Kweeta was looking at him crazy.

"So what do you think of my hair and makeup?"

You need to wash all that shit off your face and take that mop off of your head.

Basil laughed. "Oh see you trying to get me caught up. I've been around my mother and sisters enough to know that's a loaded question."

"Just speak your mind and tell the truth. It shouldn't be that hard."

"I feel like we should just end the conversation here and get back to getting to know one another."

Look at this nigga dodging the question.

"Boy bye! Stop deflecting and just answer the question. This is a part of getting to know each other."

Oh my God. How could I have missed the fact that she's so damn ghetto? Basil paused before replying, knowing that his response could send the evening into a downward spiral.

"Ok, you got me," he laughed. "I'll just say that you could be a little more polished."

Nigga you tried it! All the primping Kweeta had done before she left home and this fool was here talking about being more polished.

"How so? Is it because I'm not dressed like the rest of these stuck up broads in here?"

That's exactly it.

"Well, you are kind of standing out. And not in a good way. It's the whole get up. The nails, the pounds of hair, all the labels... let me guess, new money?"

Basil hadn't got around to asking Kweeta how she acquired her wealth but if he had to guess he would say it was either an inheritance or drug money.

"New money, old money, what the hell difference does it make? I'm not about to change who I am and how I dress just cause I got a few dollars in my pocket." Kweeta was appalled.

Basil looked around to see if anyone had heard the outburst.

"That's good to know. I need a woman that can challenge me mentally. That's well versed in politics, well traveled, has a knowledge of the arts, all while looking good on my arm. No matter where I take her she needs to look as good as me."

"Ain't that a bitch. Well how about this, I need my man to not be a pompous ass, has street smarts, as well as book smarts, with a little thug in him. Looks good in a wife beater, tatt sleeves on his arms, and won't hesitate to get crunk to protect his queen."

In that moment Kweeta realized that she'd just described Bushwick.

Basil straightened his tie. "It's obvious that we are both looking for two different things."

"Yeah, I'm sorry but I gotta keep it one hundid, you just ain't doing it for me."

Basil was flabbergasted. The nerve of this Scallywag saying that he wasn't her type.

"Sorry I'm not "hood" enough for you. I suppose if I had a few felonies and bullet wounds under my belt I would fit the bill."

Despite Basil's calloused response, his feelings were actually hurt. A man of his stature wasn't used to the rejection and it did take a bite out of him even if it were coming from a woman he was planning on rejecting down the line.

"Nah… more like if you had some class and respected women instead of trying to change them. On that note imma call it a night."

With that she chucked him the deuces, snatched a bread stick and was on her way.

****

Chapter 21- Apology Accepted

Now what could she possibly want? Zan looked at the time. *"I thought she was supposed to be on her date."*

She looked down at her phone and saw Kweeta's name on the caller ID. She thought it was odd that she would attempt to contact her after she kicked her out of her home. Her first mind told her not to answer but curiosity got the best of her.

"Hello."

"Hey it's me. I just wanted to say I'm sorry. You were right. He totally hated my outfit and said I should tone it down."

"Is that what he said?" Zan rubbed the towel through her damp hair as she listened with concern for her friend.

"Pretty much," Kweeta replied as she slid the zipper down on her boots. "I'm sorry I talked about your clothes. I guess I'm the one who needs to get some style."

One thing that Kweeta prided herself in was that when she was wrong she was woman enough to own up to her mistakes. She'd caught an attitude with Zan when all she was trying to do was help elevate her style.

"What a jerk!" Just because Zan was right it still didn't give this guy permission to tell someone how to dress. "I hope you let him have it."

Kweeta laughed as she headed to the bathroom to grab a makeup wipe.

"You already know I did. Well, I won't hold you up. I just called to apologize."

"Apology accepted. Listen, I want to apologize also. I shouldn't have tried to change who you are by telling you how to dress. Truthfully, I'm no better than that guy you went out with."

"Bullshit, you were just trying to help a sista out but I was too hot headed to appreciate it. Now don't get me wrong, imma still dress how I want but maybe we can go shopping and you can help me pick out some classier pieces to add to my wardrobe."

Zan smiled. "I would love to. And maybe you can help me loosen up a bit. I've always wanted to buy something off Fashion Nova."

"Seriously? You?"

"Yep, I wanna see what the hype is all about."

The women giggled like teenagers.

"Consider it a date," Kweeta replied.

With that they said their goodbye's and hung up. Maybe there were some cool people in Beverly Hills after all.

****

Chapter 22 – I Can Love You Better

Sedrick took another pull of his blunt to calm his nerves. He gazed at his reflection in the rearview mirror and ran his fingers across his eyebrows. Hopefully his Crown Victoria didn't stand out too much in this neighborhood. This was some fucked up shit he was about to do, but money made niggas do some strange things. He never thought it would come to this, but if he had to choose between keeping Bushwick as a lifetime friend versus living out the rest of his days in the lap of luxury, he chose the latter. Sometimes you have to make tough choices in life and this was one of them. His heart sped up as he gazed at Kweeta's house and contemplated how he would feel if one of his boys did this shit to him.

For a brief second he thought about going back on his plan. He thought about all the years he and Bushwick had been friends. He thought about all the times Bushwick had been in his corner. Finally he was struck with the realization that he wasn't shit. There was no getting around it. Bottom line there was no excuse for what he was about to do. At the end of the day the desire to be rich overruled loyalty. His only hurdle was making sure Kweeta chose him. No doubt it was going to be a task, she most likely still had feelings for Bushwick. It was going to be up to him to show her that he was everything his little ass wasn't. He checked to see if the coast was clear Before cruising up the winding driveway. He took time to gather his wits as he exited the vehicle.

"Who is it?" Kweeta asked.

"Hey Kweeta it's me Sedrick."

Kweeta cracked open the door.

"Hey Sed, Bushwick isn't here."

Kweeta wasn't sure what Sedrick wanted but she was sure it had something to do with her and Bushwick breaking up. It didn't surprise her one bit that Bushwick would send his boy over here to plead his case and try to get them back together. Little did she know she was about to get the surprise of her life.

"How you doing Kweeta? You looking beautiful today. Yeah I heard he moved out. I just stopped by to talk to you for a second. Sorry about popping up unannounced. I hope this is a good time."

His eyes shot past her, praying Bushwick wasn't there.

"Sure, come on in. Is everything ok?" She invited him in against her better judgement.

Suddenly it hit her. Maybe something happened to Bushwick.

"Bushwick isn't in any kind of trouble is he?"

"No... nothing like that. Bushwick is fine. I didn't come here to talk about him."

By now Kweeta was thoroughly confused.

"Okay.... come on in and have a seat. Can I get you anything?"

A Bentley GT convertible and the deed to this house.

"I'll take a bottle of water if you have it. This sure is a beautiful home."

Sedrick swooned over the luxurious architecture. The mere thought of going back to his raggedy ass two bedroom flat pissed him off to no end. Why should a little nigga like Bushwick have all the fun? Hell, he wanted to be laid up in the lap of luxury his damn self.

Kweeta disappeared and reemerged with two bottles of Essentia.

"So what's this all about?"

Sedrick's eyes roamed over Kweeta's voluptuous frame. His gaze lingered at the cleavage from her DDD cups peeking out the top of her shirt.

"I heard about you and Bushwick calling the engagement off."

Kweeta's face dropped at the mere thought of her not walking down the aisle with her soulmate.

"Yeah… we kinda just grew apart," she replied, fighting back the tears.

"I hate to hear that. It be like that sometimes. I just wanted to let you know that you cool with me and if you or Bugatti need anything I got you."

"That's nice of you Sed, but I'm good."

"Don't knock it. We all need somebody in our corner when we going through something."

He took a few swallows of his water before moving to the sofa where she was sitting and plopped down next to her.

By now Kweeta's gut told her that he was here for more than just to see if she was ok. She scooted over to put more space between them.

"Where are you going with this?"

"I'm just saying, I know it gets lonely being up in this big house all by yourself while baby girl is at school. I might not have much to offer by way of finances but I'm a damn good listener if you ever want to talk."

I know this fool ain't trying to be slick and ease is way up in here. The encounter was making her feel uneasy and it was time for ole boy to bounce.

She stood from her seat and started walking towards the entrance.

"Alright well, I appreciate you stopping by. If I need to talk I will let you know."

"We can do more than talk. I can take care of any other needs you might have," he bellowed in a low tone as he walked up behind her and slid his hands around her waist.

"What the hell do you think you doing?" Kweeta spat as she pushed him away.

"Come on girl don't be like that. I know that nigga wasn't taking care of your needs like I can," he replied, cupping the bottom of her ass cheek where it met the thigh.

This was a bold ass move on his part but he figured he didn't want to waste time with formalities seeing as Bushwick could come out of hiding any day. Except when he came back this time there would be another rooster in the hen house.

"Nigga have you lost your damn mind!" Kweeta screeched. "Get the fuck out my damn house!"

***

"Look Kweeta, I know I messed up but I love you and I don't want to be with nobody else." Bushwick practiced what he was going to say to Kweeta when he confronted her about them getting back together.

"Why am I so damn nervous?" *Cause you scared she might not take yo' dumb ass back.*

Bushwick had been at some low points in his life and living without Kweeta ranked at the top. It had nothing to do with her newly acquired wealth. Yeah, the money was nice but he missed his queen. She was his ride or die and he was not about to lose her behind this bullshit. While they were apart he had time to do some soul searching and realized that he needed to grow the fuck up and get his shit together. Not just for his relationship, but for himself and for his daughter. Once he rounded the corner to the block with their house he slowed down to a cruise and thought about what he would do if she didn't take him back. He found himself choking up at the thought of having to live the rest of his life without her. Once he approached the property he began ascending the long driveway. His attention was soon drawn to the car parked in front of the house.

"What the fuck! I know this nigga Sedrick ain't over here!"

He pulled up to a screeching halt, grabbed his heat and jumped out of the vehicle. He walked up just in time to see Kweeta yanking the door open and pushing Sedrick out.

"Bitch don't put yo' hands on me!"

"What the fuck is going on here! Kweeta, you creeping with this nigga!" Bushwick fumed.

Shit just got real, Sedrick thought. *Time to come up with a quick lie and get the fuck out of dodge.*

"Hell no! He popped his ass up over here pretending like he wanted to talk and made a pass at me. I was throwing his ass out!"

"Say what? Nigga, you tried to push up on my girl?" Bushwick squared off with Sed glaring up at him with flared nostrils.

"Man, don't believe that bullshit. She's the one that invited me over talking about she needed a shoulder to cry on. I felt sorry for her ass cause I knew that was ya girl. Next thing I know she all up on me. When I rejected her she put me out."

"Not today Satan! Bushwick this nigga ain't yo' friend. He knew we broke up and tried to take your place. Talking 'bout he can take care of me better than you. Nigga felt on my ass and I kicked him the fuck out!"

"Bitch please! Ain't nobody want yo' big ass! Lookin' like Kevin Durant in a lacefront."

"No his bitch ass didn't!" Kweeta spat as she took off her earrings.

"Nigga don't you ever disrespect the mother of my child!"

"Man, you gon' let this trick come between our friendship?"

No sooner than the words fell from his lips Kweeta delivered an uppercut to his chin.

"Bitch are you crazy?" Sedrick went to swing back and was met by four body blows to his stomach by Bushwick.

"Ugh!" Sedrick doubled over in pain and Kweeta jumped in the air and came down on the back of his neck with her forearm.

Damn! This big bitch tryin' to break a nigga's back.

"Fuck you and this leprechaun!" Sedrick delivered a stiff right hook to Bushwick knocking him backwards before slapping Kweeta so hard he left a mark.

In a flash Bushwick was back on his feet. Sedrick swung and Bushwick ducked him before lunging at his legs, sweeping his feet out from under him. Before Sedrick could gain his composure Bushwick had pulled his weapon and trained it at his head. Sedrick raised his hands.

"Nigga you come and disrespect my house and my fiancée. I'm 'bout to blast yo' ass!"

"Come on man…. over a female. You know me and you go way back," Sed replied nervously.

"Bushwick no! He's not worth it!" Kweeta cried out.

"Stand the fuck up!" Spit flew from Bushwick's mouth as he contemplated blowing this nigga's brains out.

Tears fell from Sedrick's eyes as he slowly stood to his feet.

"Man I swear…."

"Shut the fuck up!"

"Don't do it Bushwick!" Kweeta pleaded.

"Turn around and walk!"

"I'm your best friend."

"Bushwick ain't got no friends!" With that he let off several rounds.

"Bushwick no!!" Kweeta yelped.

Sedrick's knees buckled as he raced towards his car and jumped in.

Bushwick emptied the clip, blowing out Sed's back tire. "Big Draco nigga!"

Sedrick peeled out, burning rubber. The back rim sparked as it drug along the concrete.

Once Bushwick realized what he'd done he took off just in time to miss the police.

"This is exactly why I can't be with this nigga," Kweeta reflected as she picked up the shells from the driveway.

This had been a crazy ass day.

****

Chapter 23 – Betrayal

Bushwick's heart slammed against his ribcage. This entire experience had been mind blowing.

"What the fuck!"

He quickly placed the steel piece under his seat and focused on maintaining the speed limit. The last thing he needed was the cops pulling him over and finding a gun. His eyes darted back-and-forth from the road to his rearview mirror to see if he was being followed. He was almost at the hotel when an unmarked police car began trailing him.

"Shit!"

"I cannot go back to jail. I'll never get my family back."

The car followed behind him for several blocks, if he had to take a guess he would say that they were probably running his plates. Lucky for him he had his shit in order. All he needed to do now was just play it cool. When he got to the next red light the car pulled up beside him. The driver was a middle-aged African-American man. He glanced over at Bushwick and gave him a nod.

"Thank you Jesus." Bushwick looked up at the sky.

Once he arrived at his destination he made sure that the coast was clear before tucking the gun in his waistband and heading inside.

"I gotta get rid of this shit."

Now that he was in the clear his attention was focused back on Sedrick and Kweeta.

"My boy and my muthafuckin woman. This some bullshit." He snarled as he hurled the lamp off the table.

The mere thought of those two messing around behind his back was enough to drive him insane. He believed Kweeta. But there was still that shadow of a doubt of wondering what he walked up on.

"Why the fuck would she let him in?"

Would Sedrick be so bold as to push up on his girl as soon as he found out they broke up? He had known this nigga all his life. Let him tell it, Kweeta was the one that came on to him. Everything inside of him wanted to believe her. But he also didn't want to be made a fool. The idea of the two people closest to him betraying him cut him deeply. Even if Kweeta was telling the truth. Losing a friend still hurt. Bottom line, if that nigga was lying he deserved one of the muthafuckin bullets to hit his ass. Aside from going to jail, a part of Bushwick still didn't know if Kweeta was telling the complete truth therefore he purposely missed Sedrick with his aim. That, and the fact that he didn't have the heart to kill someone who was once like a brother to him.

He picked up the pieces of shattered glass off the floor then cracked open the bottle of Henny he'd been nursing the past few days.

He took several gulps before taking his shoes off and laying crossways the bed.

When has Kweeta ever lied to you? That's your queen. You were about to marry this woman. In the whole time that you've known her Kweeta has never given you any reason to think she was stepping out.

He took comfort in the notion that Kweeta still loved him and wouldn't betray his trust. Minutes later he dozed off. After sleeping for about 30 minutes he was awakened by his mind racing with images of Sedrick and Kweeta having sex. He sat up on the side of the bed and took two more swigs from his bottle. The more he tried to push this shit out of his mind the more it consumed him.

Don't be a damn fool man. You done known Sedrick since y'all was kids. Would he really stoop this low to do some shit like this?

"Fuck I don't know who to trust."

Trust your gut. You know that nigga lying. Why would she want his ass? It ain't like he got shit to offer.

"Hell yeah, I'm trippin. Kweeta don't want his punk ass. I mean shit, she's rich now. She can have any man she wants. Why the fuck would she want a broke ass nigga from the hood?"

Each time he toyed with the idea of Kweeta telling the truth, negative thoughts soon raced in his head to replace the positive ones.

Hello? You're a broke ass nigga from the hood and she wanted you.

Bushwick felt like he was losing his damn mind. He drank himself into a stupor and passed out.

****

Chapter 24 - Missing Him

The warm sun felt good on Kweeta's skin as she laid back and sipped her Mai Tai. Zan had invited her and Cherokee over to relax by the pool. No matter how hard she tried she couldn't get Bushwick off of her mind. She thought about all the good times they shared together, and she thought about all the rough times they shared together. And how he always had her back no matter what. One of the things that hurt her the most was the fact that she thought she would never find a man that she would be as close to as Bushwick. Before she knew it her memories consumed her. Tears began to stream down her cheeks. The harder she tried to choke them back the faster they fell. She thought about how he had fought for her the week before.

"What's the matter sweetie?" Zan asked, noticing that her friend was in distress.

"She's probably upset because they cut her food stamps off," Cherokee joked.

She was low-key pissed at the fact Zan had taken it upon herself to add Kweeta to their circle. She didn't care for her and she made no qualms about showing it.

Kweeta pretended that she didn't hear the remark. If she would've caught her at any other time she would've caught a beat down. But right now this trick wasn't worth her energy.

"Must you be a bitch all the time?" Zan fussed.

"Whatever," Cherokee waived off the comment. "I'm out. I have more pressing business." On her way out of the yard she mumbled to Zan. "When you're tired of slumming, call me later."

By now Zan was totally ignoring her, she sat beside Kweeta and offered tissue and words of comfort.

"Don't pay her any attention. Now are you going to tell me what's bothering you?"

"I miss Bushwick," Kweeta sniffled. "I've never been away from him for this long."

"Aww sweetie, you still love him don't you?"

"Of course I still love him. We were together for four years. He was my one true love. My feelings for him aren't going away that easily. We had that Remy and Papoose type of love."

"So why are you moping around here? Girl, call that man up and tell him how you feel."

****

Chapter 25 – Back Where He Belongs

"So, I'm just saying, we need to talk."

"Say no more. I'm on my way."

It had been exactly four months since Bushwick and Kweeta had split. Up until this point their attempts at trying to patch up their relationship failed because neither of them wanted to back down. Although Bushwick realized that he was wrong for how he'd been acting, he still entertained the notion that something may have happened between her and Sed.

When he arrived at the house he let out a deep sigh. He had to admit it felt glorious being back home. He was willing to do whatever it took to make it work.

"Hey," Kweeta greeted him with a warm smile.

"Hey, I'm glad you called me."

"Come on in, you hungry?"

"Only if you already cooked. I don't want you to go out of your way."

"I made your favorite, smothered porkchops."

"That's what I'm talkin' 'bout! You know exactly what I like."

Bushwick hadn't eaten a home cooked meal since he and Kweeta broke up. That eating out shit was getting old.

He was just about to ask where Bugatti was when she came running into the kitchen.

"Daddy!"

The child ran to him and put her arms around him.

"Hey baby girl!" He gave her a tight squeeze. "I missed you."

"I missed you too. Are you and mama getting back together?"

Bushwick looked at Kweeta.

"We gon' see. Your daddy came by so we can talk." Kweeta didn't want to make the child any promises.

That seemed to be enough to satisfy Bugatti for the time being. She released her embrace and ran to the dinner table. "What's for dinner?"

"Smothered porkchops, you and your daddy's favorite."

For the first time in months the trio sat around the table as a family and had dinner. Kweeta was overcome with emotion seeing them back together. She began to sniffle. She turned her head to wipe the tear that was about to drop.

"What's wrong mama?"

"Nothing baby, just happy to see my family together."

Bushwick placed his hand over Kweeta's.

When the meal was over Bugatti excused herself so they could talk.

"Let me start…. Bushwick, I never thought of you as less of a man because you couldn't buy me the same things I was buying you. And this house is just as much yours…."

"Hold up Kweeta, let me stop you. You don't need to explain any of that. It's been me trippin the whole time."

"Say what?" Kweeta couldn't believe her ears. Bushwick was finally taking accountability for his actions.

Bushwick laughed. "You should see the look on your face. But in all seriousness, I fucked up. I let my insecurities get the best of me. I'm not gon' lie and say that it still doesn't bother me that I can't provide for you and Bugatti. A real man always wants to take care of his home. But imma stop acting like a dumb ass every time you want to help me. And imma figure out a way to get my own, legally."

Kweeta breathed a sigh of relief.

"I'm so happy to hear you say that. Lord knows I don't know what I'll do if you go back to jail."

"I'm not going back. All that shit is behind me."

"Even your temper? Bushwick I know you always want to protect me but you can't be running around busting caps every time somebody pisses you off."

"True 'dat, but that nigga Sed had it coming." His facial expression changed upon the mention of his name.

"Speaking of Sedrick, come here I want to show you something."

Kweeta led Bushwick over to the security monitor. She then pulled up the footage for the day that Sedrick stopped by. Once she got to the part with him standing outside the door she rewound it and turned up the volume.

"Look Kweeta you don't have to do this…"

"Shhhh, just listen."

"Hey Sed Bushwick isn't here."

"How you doing Kweeta? You looking beautiful today. Yeah I heard he moved out. I just stopped by to talk to you for a second. Sorry about popping up unannounced. I hope this is a good time."

"He lied, I never invited him over. He showed up unannounced. It was stupid of me to let him in thinking that he just wanted to talk."

"That lying bastard. I wanna beat his ass all over again."

Despite his mind playing tricks on him, in his heart Bushwick knew Kweeta wouldn't betray him but it still felt good seeing proof.

"I'm not gon' lie, that shit fucked with me for a minute. I'm pissed that I even entertained that shit. You a good ass woman Kweeta. And I know you ain't trippin' off trying to please white folks. I was just talkin' shit cause we got kicked out and a nigga's ego was bruised. But the truth is, niggas do need to grow up. Can you forgive me for being so stupid?"

"I forgive you. Let's make a promise that we won't let anything get in the way of our happiness."

"I promise."

When it was all said and done they talked about all the issues concerning their relationship. Kweeta even told Bushwick about her date seeing as she didn't want to keep any secrets from him. The end result was them agreeing to get back together.

"I love you Bushwick."

"I love you too baby."

Their lips met for a tender kiss.

Bugatti crept to the doorway and smiled. Her daddy was finally coming back home.

****

Chapter 26 – Do Me Baby

Kweeta tousled her hair a bit before applying a few sprays of Versace Bright Crystal. She slipped on a pair of Louboutin stilettos before adjusting the strap on her garter. She'd been craving Bushwick's touch for weeks and now that her man was finally back home where he belonged it was time to put it on him. She gazed at her reflection, admiring how the sheer black teddy showcased every curve.

"Damn.." Bushwick said under his breath as she entered the room carrying two glasses of Moet.

"You like?" she asked, handing him a glass.

"I more than like it. I'm 'bout to sop yo' fine ass up like a biscuit in some gravy," he salivated as he took the glass from her.

Kweeta's heart fluttered at the compliment. She took a seat next to him on the loveseat and crossed her lengthy toned legs. Bushwick took a sip from his glass and sat it down. The past few months of sleeping alone were some of the loneliest nights of his life. He'd never been away from his bae this long and if he could help it, he would never be away from her again. He wasted no time diving right in. As soon as they started kissing he went from semi hard to a full on erection. Their tongues danced in each other's mouth as he groped her breast. A soft moan escaped her lips as his teeth grazed over her hardened nipples through the sheer fabric.

Moments later his face was between her silky thighs. He inhaled her essence before wrapping his lips around her erect clit. She arched her back in ecstasy as he slid two fingers inside of her.

"Oooh, that feels so good baby," she panted.

His tongue traced her swollen lips before finding it's way to her center, replacing his fingers. He gripped her hips with both hands lifting her ass in the air as he continued to thrust his tongue. Within minutes she climaxed.

After regaining her composure she was ready to return the favor.

"Your turn daddy," she cooed as she walked him over to the bed. "Lay back."

He was already rock hard. She was about to take him in her mouth when he directed her to get on top of him.

"That can wait. I want to be inside of you right now," he growled.

"Your wish is my command," she purred.

After straddling him she lowered herself onto the hardness of his manhood. This is what she had been waiting for. Bushwick may have been a man of short stature but he more than made up for it with the log between his legs.

"Hell yeah, just like that. Damn I missed these long legs," Bushwick moaned as he rubbed the silky stockings.

Kweeta found her rhythm and began sliding up and down on him. Bushwick began thrusting hard, enjoying every minute of being inside her tight, slippery walls. Kweeta could feel his dick pulsing inside her and it drove her nuts. It felt so good she began bouncing up and down on him wildly.

"Ooh, that's my spot!" She moaned.

Bushwick didn't even attempt to hold back. Kweeta's wetness felt so good wrapped around his meat that he couldn't if he wanted to. Seconds later both of their bodies shuddered as they came for what seemed like an eternity. She collapsed on top of him and they shared a kiss. It didn't take long for him to start getting hard again. He stood up on his knees and directed Kweeta to do the same. He slapped her firm ass before entering her from behind. He reached around and groped her tits as he rocked her pelvis. Kweeta teased her clit as she bounced her ass back against him, matching his rhythm.

"Fuck..," Bushwick groaned under his breath.

His knees almost buckled as he buried himself deep inside of her. Kweeta bit her lip to stifle her screams as she tightened her walls around him. Bushwick wrapped her hair in his fist and arched her back for leverage as he thrusted aggressively. Kweeta felt the heat rising inside of her. A roar of passion tore from her throat as she lost control. When her thighs finally stopped trembling she pulled herself away from Bushwick who was now close to exploding. His balls tightened as she stroked him with both hands before taking him into her throat. She slid up and down tasting her wetness on him. Seconds later he shuddered and spilled his seed. Kweeta swallowed every drop. They crashed on the bed in exhaustion and fell asleep in each other's arms.

****

Chapter 27 - Busted

Austin's face twisted into a scowl as he flip through the pages.

What the fuck is this?

Zan had accidentally left her budgeting notebook out on the counter. Normally this wouldn't be a problem. But seeing as it included the money she had been giving to Cherokee, all hell was about to break loose.

There were dates going back for several months where Cherokee's name was listed with a dollar amount beside it.

Cherokee $2000.

Cherokee $500.

Cherokee $1000.

Austin felt his blood beginning to boil.

"ALEXENDRIA! What the hell is this?"

"What is he down there fussing about now?" Zan said as she wound off several inches of dental floss.

Austin climbed the stairs two at a time. His blood pressure banged against his skull.

I know this sneaky bitch is not getting money from my wife.

"Zan what is this?" He asked tossing the notebook down in front of her.

"So you just snooping through my shit now?"

"I wasn't snooping through shit. You left it out on the counter. Why is Cherokee's name in here with a dollar amount beside it?" He glared at her waiting for a response.

Oh shit! I didn't mean for him to see that.

The stunned look on Zan's face confirmed Austin's suspicions.

"I…. I gave her money a few times."

"So we're just passing out money without telling each other?"

"I'm sorry. I know I should have talked to you first. It's just that she was in a bind and needed our help."

"Fuck that bitch!" Austin seethed.

"I know you're angry babe, but the girl needed help."

"Please, that bitch is a groupie thot. Let one of her men help her. That's not your job."

Wait till I see this triflin ass bitch.

Zan knew he would be pissed if he found out but he didn't have to be so insensitive.

"Cut her some slack. She's just going through a rough patch."

"Rough patch my ass. We are not about to support the lifestyle of a lazy ass thot who refuses to work."

Austin was heated but he knew Zan's heart was in the right place. Little did she know that he had been giving Cherokee money for the past year as well.

Zan let out a sigh. "I know…"

As much as she hated to admit it, Austin was right.

"Promise me you won't give her any more money. And you will come to me first before helping someone else out."

"I promise."

Before she finished speaking Austin was on his way downstairs.

"Where are you going?" Zan yelled out.

"Running a few errands. I'll be back in a few."

Austin knew he was taking a major risk going to see Cherokee in broad daylight but this shit couldn't wait. He needed to check this bitch right now.

After driving a few blocks over and parking his car, he hopped out and took off on foot. When he got to his street he made his way to the back entrance of Cherokee's house. He used the security code to let himself in the gate. Once he was inside he banged on her back door.

"Who the hell is that?" Cherokee had just stepped out of the shower when she heard the banging at her back door. She wrapped a robe around her and made her way to the security monitor. It was Austin.

"What's he doing here?" She wasn't expecting him but she was damn sure letting him in. Maybe he had a change of heart about giving her some loot. She quickly made her way downstairs and opened the door.

"You had a change of heart Papi?"

"Cut the bullshit Cherokee. You been taking money from my wife?" He already knew the truth. He just wanted to see if the bitch was going to admit it.

Oh shit, Cherokee could feel her heart leaping in her chest. The gig was up.

"I mean yeah, I borrowed money from her once."

"Once my ass. You've been getting money from her for the past few months. And you been getting money from me. You truly ain't shit. The way you smile in my wife's face while fucking her husband behind her back. And the nerve of you to take money from both of us. You're about as sorry as they come."

This pissed Cherokee off. The nerve of this nigga. *I know his punk ass is not trying to check me.*

She rushed out to the back patio where he was standing and jumped in his face.

"You got a lot of nerve muthafucka! You forget it takes two to tango."

Before she knew it, Austin snapped and grabbed her by her neck.

"Bitch, don't you ever fucking disrespect me like that. Like I said before. I gave you a little money here and there because I felt sorry for you. But just like the groupie trollop you are, you had to go and get greedy. You ain't never had shit. And you ain't gonna never be shit unless it's a man taking care of you."

Tears and snot ran down Cherokee's beet red face as she struggled to regain her composure.

"Fuck you, you sorry son of a bitch! You're just as much at fault as me."

"Miss me with the bullshit," Austin spat as he began walking away.

"How dare you put your hands on me. You just wait. Imma have something for yo' punk ass! I'm not the one who made a commitment to your wife. I hope she leaves your sorry ass," Cherokee screamed as she raced behind him.

Austin spun around in a fury. He gritted his teeth as he delivered a stiff back hand across her face knocking her into the pool.

"Stay the fuck away from my wife and stay the fuck away from me!"

Chapter 28 – Face The Truth

"So where this corny nigga live."

"He lives on my street but you can't get to him there. It's too risky. Maybe catch him going to his car after work. He works late quite often."

Cherokee called in a favor from Tank, one of her hood cousins who'd just did a bid for armed robbery.

"He carry any loot on him? You know rich people only use cards."

"Not that I know of but he does wear a Rolex and a diamond wedding band. And he has several luxury vehicles. He usually takes the Benz to work."

"Wedding ring huh?" Tank smirked before taking a sip of his soda.

"Look, don't judge. You wanna make this loot or not?"

Tank threw his hands in the air. "I'm not judging, do you baby girl. You had me at the Rolie and the Benz," he replied before cramming his mouth full of fries.

"So we have a deal?"

"I'm in. I need this lick. Plus you know I don't play about a nigga putting his hands on my baby cousin."

Cherokee sat back in her seat and breathed a sigh of relief. Austin had her all the way fucked up if he thought he was going to short change her and put his hands on her. Her first thought was to call the police and blow up his spot but she didn't need the negative press, especially with her trying to get her career off the ground. Once they were done eating she paid the bill and they parted ways.

Cherokee slid on her Givenchy shades and pulled the hoodie down over her forehead before she emerged to the parking lot. If she didn't need to see Tank in person she wouldn't have left the house. Her plan was to stay inside until the purplish green handprint around her neck and the welt on her left cheek had fully disappeared. As she raced to her car she suddenly heard footsteps behind her.

"Cherokee?"

FUCK! It was Zan. This was the last person she wanted to see right now. She'd managed to avoid her the past few days.

"Hey Zan," Cherokee spun around and replied abruptly before resuming her trek to her vehicle.

"Slow down. Where are you off to in such a rush? I've been trying to get in touch with you. Why did you stand me up yesterday? I thought we agreed to play tennis at 2pm," Zan replied as she walked briskly alongside her.

"Huh? Oh… something came up. I forgot to text you. Sorry."

As she attempted to get in her car Zan stopped her.

"What's going on? Why are you acting so strange?"

"Just tired. I had a long night. Listen I gotta run. I'll call you later."

Zan wasn't buying it. By now she had not only noticed her weird behavior, she thought it was off for her to be hiding under a hoodie in eighty five degree weather. Especially as much as Cherokee loved flaunting her body. On a normal day she would be damn near naked. Something was definitely off. Upon closer inspection she noticed the red mark on her face that she unsuccessfully attempted to cover with makeup.

"What is that on your face?" Zan shrieked as she pulled back Cherokee's hood. "Did someone hit you?"

"Could you not! I told you I'm in a hurry!" Cherokee snatched away from her.

"To hell with that! I'm not letting you leave until you tell me which one of those losers put his hands on you."

It was obvious that Zan wasn't going to give it a rest. Cherokee figured that she better think of a story quick if she wanted to get rid of her. She held the hoodie tight around her neck as she responded.

"If you must know, I had a date with a fuck boy last night and we got into a little spat. I'm ok though. Now can I please go?"

Zan's gut told her the she wasn't telling her everything.

"What an asshole! Are you sure you're ok? Why are you holding that shirt like that?"

What the fuck! Get a life bitch!

Zan pulled at the neck of Cherokee's hoodie, exposing the bruising around her neck.

"What the hell Cherokee? Who did this to you? Have you gone to the police?"

"No! I told you I can't talk right now!"

It was obvious that Cherokee had taken a beat down and was afraid to speak up. This enraged Zan. It was bad enough that she was going through all this bullshit with the house, and now this. What type of friend would she be if she just left her without at least getting her to the police station?

Zan stepped in front of Cherokee's door. I'm not moving until you say who did this or you at least agree to go to the police. Did that son of a bitch threaten you not to tell anyone?"

Seeing the concern Zan had for Cherokee's wellbeing actually made her feel bad. She looked at her with tears in her eyes.

"Look, I haven't gone to the police yet but I plan on filing a report today. I just popped out to grab a cup of coffee and reflect on the whole situation."

"Oh, honey, I'm so sorry... you know you could have called me." Zan gave her a brief embrace.

"I know but I kinda just wanted to be alone. We'll talk later, I promise."

Zan wasn't totally sold on the exchange but it was enough to back her down and send her on her way.

****

Chapter 29 – Don't Let The Doorknob Hit You

"I don't think their yard is up to code either," Mrs. Dickerson sneered.

"It's not! I know for a fact those big tacky ass lions they have at the entrance of the property aren't a part of the community standards. Not to mention they are a friggin eyesore," Austin agreed. It was his month to lead the Housing Association meeting. The first order of business, getting rid of Kweeta and Bushwick.

Several of the other neighbors chimed in.

"My word! Aren't they absolutely ghastly?" said Kweeta's neighbor Mrs. Dickerson. "They are going to make all of our property value go down."

"Yes they are Mrs. Dickerson. That's why we are here to do something about it," Austin reassured her.

"I will admit when they first moved in my husband and I thought they were relatives of yours," Mrs. Dickerson admitted. "My apologies," she added.

"Absolutely not!" Austin was outraged at the implication. "Those vagabonds are of no relation to me or my wife."

Zan rolled her eyes at her husband for being the ring leader in this foolishness. This stupid motherfucker didn't have sense enough to realize that they were saying all black people look alike.

"I could have sworn I heard gunshots coming from over there but I can't prove it," Dalton Ewald added.

"I heard it too Dalton," old man Pierce and his wife Judith agreed.

Zan sucked her teeth at all the faux pearl clutching.

"And they play that trap music really loud." Judith said raising a shaky hand.

"How do you know what trap music is Judith?" Zan asked raising an eyebrow.

"I heard the young black fellow say he was going to the trap so I Googled it."

Bullshit, your old ass is probably listening to it your damn self.

"Y'all got a lot of nerve talking about people when they aren't here to defend themselves."

Austin cringed at Zan's outburst. And why the hell was she still trying to defend these hoodrats when it was clear that everyone wanted them out of the neighborhood?

"Zan, honey…. I don't think you should speak on matters that you know nothing about. It's obvious that everyone seems to be having a problem with them." He gave her a warning glance to back down. A threat that she didn't take kindly too.

"Everyone like who? These few old bittys sitting here? They don't speak for the entire community."

"We do if we are the only ones to show up to the meetings," Judith clapped back.

"That's where you are wrong dear," he replied in a condescending tone. He turned to Judith. "You are absolutely right. Someone has to take the initiative to care about the neighborhood even if no one else does," he said glaring at Zan. "If we let those heathens have their way what's next? Bandos on every corner? I've been checking out the urban dictionary myself." He winked at Judith and tapped the side of his head.

"Unfucking believable! We don't know anything about these people. They haven't caused any more trouble than anyone else on the block. They mind their business and stay to themselves for the most part. I'm not sitting here agreeing to this racist bullshit," Zan protested.

What a shit show. And the sad part is, my husband is the ring leader.

The patrons of the meeting turned to Austin for answers.

"Please excuse my wife. She's having a bit of PMS right now."

Everyone mumbled amongst themselves and nodded their heads.

What an asshole!

"Fuck you Austin!" Zan spat and stormed out of the meeting.

When they got back to the house Zan got out of the car and slammed the door so hard she almost tore it off the hinges.

"Don't ever in your life fucking embarrass me again the way you did back there," Zan raged.

Austin laughed out loud. "Ha! Embarrass you? You know what? You're a joke Zan."

"No, the joke is you shucking and jiving for people who don't give a damn about you. Your dumb ass really thinks that just because we live in this neighborhood you are one of them. Well I got news for you Austin, you're not. In their eyes you're still the same nigga from the hood."

Austin turned his nose up at the words Zan spoke.

"You disgust me."

Zan had secretly put up with Austin's verbal abuse over the past few years but for some reason those words cut her to the core. To have the man that she was supposed to spend the rest of her life with tell her that he was disgusted by her made her feel lower than dirt. His mission was accomplished.

Tears filled Zan's eyes. "I don't know who you are anymore. You're damn sure not the man I married."

"One of us had to grow in the relationship since the other one insists on slumming. I didn't work my ass off to move out of the fucking ghetto to remember. I moved out to forget. You "sistas", he put up the quotation signs with his two fingers. Always yapping about a black man getting rich then marrying white women. Well this is why. Y'all don't know how to appreciate shit. Maybe I should've married one."

He didn't actually believe those words but he knew they would hurt her.

Zan became infuriated. She slapped Austin across his face. "Fuck you asshole!"

This was the first time she'd ever put her hands on him but she had about all she could take. She was at her breaking point.

"Bitch…" Austin slapped her back and grabbed her by her hair dragging her over to the bed. She grunted and cried out as he held her hair tight with one hand. He was about to let out a fury of punches with the other when Bianca walked into their room crying.

"Mommy are you ok?"

Austin released his grip and shook his hands as he turned his back. He couldn't face his baby girl at the moment.

"It's ok baby. Do me a favor, go down to Bugatti's house and ask her mommy can you sit down there for a little while. I'll be down there to pick you up as soon as me and your daddy are done talking."

Bianca ran to her room and grabbed a few of her dolls and the house key before heading down to her friend's house.

"You see that shit?" Austin seethed. This is all your fault. That ghetto shit has spilled over into our house. I told you to stop hanging with that gutter rat. Now you go and send our child down there."

"Kweeta has nothing to do with this. As a matter of fact she's been a better friend to me than Cherokee."

No shit dumbass.

"Are you really that stupid or is it a joke? You are so fucking naïve that you didn't realize you had a snake right under your damn nose. You're so freaking gullible that you believe in the good in everybody. Cherokee is a fucking lowlife just like Kweeta. The bitch was getting money from me the same time she was getting it from you."

In Austin's anger he spoke too soon. He didn't mean to reveal the fact that he'd also been giving Cherokee money.

Fuck it. What's she gon' do?

Zan's hands begin to shake at the possible answer to the next question she was about to ask.

"So you mean to tell me that it was a problem for me to give her money? But you gave her money? When was this?"

A smile spread across Austin's face as he ignored Zan and began putting on his shoes "Man I'm done with this shit."

On the contrary, Zan was far from done with it. Any other time she would have let it rest but she had time today.

"I asked you a fucking question. When did you give her money?" There was no way she was letting this shit slide especially the way he came at her when she told him she was helping her.

Who the hell does she think she's checking?

"Every time she sucked my dick." Austin stated smugly before heading downstairs.

At that point Zan lost it. She marched in the kitchen and snatched a butchers knife off the block and proceeded to lunge after him. "You sorry piece of shit! She yelled flailing the knife in the air.

Austin managed to dodge the blade. His attempts at trying to restrain her wrists were useless. Zan had turned into a mad woman. She swung the knife wildly slashing him on his shoulder. He touched the spot where the blood gushed from and looked up at her with fear in his eyes.

"You're crazy!"

"You haven't seen crazy. I'll kill you asshole! She lunged at him again, this time he was able to knock the blade from her hand and delivered a blow to the jaw.

Zan sat on the floor defeated, holding her face. "Get your shit and get the fuck out of this house!"

****

Chapter 30 – Fairweather Friend

"What the hell?" Kweeta fussed.

Someone was ringing the doorbell like crazy.

"If this is a damn solicitor I'm cussing they ass out."

She looked out the door and didn't see anyone. That is until she glanced down and saw Bianca.

"Bianca girl, what's wrong with you ringing my doorbell like that? Where is your ma…" Before Kweeta could finish she noticed the girl was clearly distraught. "Bianca? Baby what's wrong? Come on in."

At this point she was sobbing so hard she could barely speak. My….My mommy."

"Oh my God! Did something happen to your mama?"

At this point Bugatti came out of her room and stood at the balcony overhead.

"My daddy and my mom are fighting. She wanted to know if I could come sit down here. She said she would come and get me." With that she shook with tears.

"Oh baby I'm so sorry." Kweeta wrapped her arms around the child and led her to the sofa. Are you ok? Did that muthafucka put his hands on you?"

"What's going on?" Bushwick asked upon hearing all the commotion.

"Bianca says her parents are fighting. Zan had her come down here."

"Word? Do we need to go down there and open a can of whoop ass?" Bushwick was ready to jump into action.

Bugatti came downstairs to console her friend.

"No Bushwick. That's the last thing we need to do. We don't need you getting into any more trouble. But we do need to send the police down there in case he's hurting her."

If this were any other time she would have had her blade ready to cut a bitch. But seeing as Bushwick would most likely follow suit and have her back, she figured it was better to let the po po's handle this one. Not to mention both of the girls were there and she wanted to set an example in front of them. Just as Kweeta was about to grab her phone there was a knock at the door.

"Hang on let me get it," Bushwick announced. "This nigga might be coming for his kid. If that fool try to start some shit over here I got something for his ass."

He yanked open the door to see a bruised and battered Zan.

"Damn girl you all right?"

"Yes I'll be fine," Zan sniffled. "Is Bianca here?"

"Yeah, come on in." Bushwick invited her into the family room where everyone was sitting.

"Mommy…" Bianca wrapped her arms around her mother's waist and squeezed her tightly.

"Hey baby. Mommy is ok," she replied, rubbing the back of her daughter's head.

She looked up at Kweeta. "Thank you so much for taking my baby in. We won't take up anymore of your time. Come on Bianca grab your things."

"Hold up, so are we supposed to just ignore that big ass bruise across your face. This baby came down here crying saying that y'all were fighting."

Kweeta hated getting in their business but Zan kind of put them into it by sending her kid down to her house.

"Yes, it's a long story. I'm exhausted," Zan said in a defeated tone as tears escaped her eyes.

"Do we need to call the police?" Kweeta asked.

"No, he's gone."

"But what if that bitch doubles back? Girl you need to change those locks tonight." Kweeta glanced over at the girls. "Oops, sorry." She gave Bushwick the eye to get them out of the room.

Zan agreed with what Kweeta was saying but she was just too tired to deal with all that.

"Come on, y'all want some ice cream?"

The girls both nodded and followed Bushwick to the kitchen. Once the coast was clear they resumed the conversation.

"So what happened girl?"

"It started off at the block club meeting. Austin was being a total ass. He was siding with some of the neighbors who want you guys out." Zan looked up at Kweeta teary eyed. "I'm sorry, I told them that you guys don't bother anyone and you need to stay."

That rat bastard, Bushwick said that nigga wasn't shit. Damn! That's messed up. I'm glad you were there to speak up on our behalf. Is that what set him off?"

"That's exactly what set him off. He started undermining me in front of everyone. When we got home we had a huge blow up." Suddenly Zan stopped talking and wept silently.

"Zan, what is it?"

"Austin has been having sex with Cherokee and giving her money."

Kweeta covered her mouth.

"What the fuck?"

"What the fuck is right. Austin has always been a jerk but I never suspected he was cheating."

"With a snake bitch that's right under your nose. Just say the word and it will be on site as soon as I see that bitch."

"I appreciate it but she's not worth it. From the looks of things someone already got to her."

"What you mean?"

"Cherokee has been dodging me lately. I know why now. Anyway, someone had banged her up pretty bad."

"Hmph, serves her ass right."

I just want to go home and relax. I'm gonna take a few days off from work and figure some things out."

"I hear you girl. Well let me know if you need anything."

"I will. Thank you again for having Bianca."

Zan left and followed Kweeta's advice and got the locks changed the next day. She would spend the remainder of her days planning her next move. Austin had his ways but he'd never been this bad. She was broken hearted and emotionally drained but one thing was certain, she refused to continue raising Bianca in a toxic environment.

****

Chapter 31- Woman To Woman

"You really are a piece of work," Zan snarled. She had a mind to snatch this bitch up and slap the taste out of her mouth but she wasn't worth it.

Cherokee had managed to successfully dodge Zan for the past few weeks. Whenever she came to her house she pretended to not be at home and she didn't answer her calls. The guilt and shame was just too much to bear. The fact that she was stepping to her meant that Austin had spilled the beans about their affair. The worse part about the entire scenario was, not only didn't she think about what her relationship with Austin would do to her and Zan's friendship if she found out, she basically didn't care. What hurt her the most was she was no longer able to get money out of either of them. Seeing as they lived on the same street, it was only a matter of time before they would run into each other. Cherokee figured she may as well face her now and get it over with. It was the least she could do seeing as Zan had help fund her lifestyle for the past few months.

"Hey Zan…. I've been meaning to call you."

"Bullshit! The only reason you are speaking to me now is because I had to track your ass down like a hawk."

No lies were told there.

"So what is it that you want from me?"

"I want an apology you slut! I fucking gave you money when no one else was willing to help. I invited you in my home, broke bread with you, paid for vacations…. And this is the thanks I get. You fuck my husband."

Cherokee could see the rage in Zan's eyes and didn't want to further set her off. She figured she'd better pull the sympathy card and hope it worked. One of the thigs she learned in being an aspiring actress was learning how to cry on cue. Time to pull that shit out now.

"Look Zan, I'm really sorry. I just got caught up. I was desperate for money and would have done anything."

"That's obvious."

"The money you were giving me wasn't enough. I decided to ask Austin but he said I had to preform favors for the cash."

"So just fuck our friendship?" Who was she kidding? Cherokee had never been a real friend. Austin was right. She'd been so naïve that she didn't realize that she had a snake sitting right under her nose.

"Zan….."

"You know what? Fuck you and Austin. I hope y'all have a happy life together. You two deserve each other."

Little to Zan's knowledge, her and Austin were no longer an item. However, she didn't bother sticking around for that part of the story.

Chapter 32- Watch Ya Back

"Check in that watch fool!"

Austin hit the ground with a thud. The cold steel pressed against the back of his head.

"What is this?" He asked raising his hands in the air. He attempted to turn his head and was met with the butt of the weapon slammed into his temple.

His punk ass done been away from the hood for so long he don't know when he getting jacked.

"Next time it's gon' be a bullet. Come up out that jewelry!"

Austin shook with fear as he undid his watch and slid off his wedding band. Despite his marriage being on the rocks, it actually hurt him to remove it from his finger.

"You got any cash fool?" The goon barked as he rummaged through his pockets.

"I have less than $200 on me. It's yours. Please, take anything you want, just don't kill me."

Austin's life flashed before his eyes as he thought about Zan and Bianca and how much of a mess he'd made of everything.

The goon snatched up the loot and his keys before unleashing a wave of blows to his head along with his size twelve timbos to his ribcage.

That's for my cuzzo fuckboy.

Austin writhed about on the ground in pain. The goon delivered one final kick to his jaw causing him to spit out teeth before taking his car and peeling out.

****

Chapter 33- Hard Lesson

"Oh I see Miss Thang got a pattern," Cherokee observed as she watched Kweeta toss her gym bag in the back of her Ferrari.

Not only did she notice that Kweeta went to the gym at the same time each day, she also took notice to the fact that Bushwick was back in the house. Since she had fucked up with Zan and Austin, Bushwick was ripe for the picking.

"His petite ass is a tenth of the size of the niggas I fuck with, but a bitch might have to give his little ass some pussy if he comes up off some coins."

She waited until the next day to make sure her assumptions weren't leading her wrong. Just like clockwork, 12:30 on the dot Kweeta was out the door. About 15 minutes later Bushwick could be seen in the driveway detailing his ride.

"Perfect," she purred.

"I think it's time for me to do a little yardwork."

She proceeded to slide on a skin tight tank and the booty shorts that showcased her BBL on full display. She then slid on some Fenty gloss and headed outside. Once she was out there she couldn't figure out what she should be doing and she felt silly so she went back inside and grabbed the broom. She pretended to sweep the leaves from her walkway making sure to bend over in Bushwick's direction every now and then. She peeked over her sunglasses several times to see if he noticed her, which he didn't.

Cherokee let out a sigh. "Time to step my game up."

She headed over to Kweeta's house switching super hard. Bushwick had on his beats headphones as he worked the white walls on his tires. He soon noticed a pair of perfectly manicured feet standing in front of him. He yanked off the headphones and looked up to see Cherokee grinning at him from ear to ear.

"Hi, I don't believe we have met. I'm your neighbor Cherokee." She extended her hand towards him

Bushwick stood to his feet and wiped his hand off on his pants leg before shaking her hand. "Nice to meet you."

"I know you guys haven't been here that long. What do you think of the neighborhood so far?"

Damn I sound dumb as hell.

Bushwick paused a second before responding. There was a bit of skepticism on his part seeing as she never spoke to him before. He was curious as to the real reason for her visit. Especially since Kweeta had expressed that she really didn't care for her.

"It's ok. We like it well enough I guess."

"Ok well I just wanted to stop by and introduce myself and say hello."

"Ooookay," Bushwick was puzzled. "It was nice to meet you."

"It was nice meeting you too Bushwick."

Oh my God could you have fucked that up any worse? Don't give up just yet girl you can always salvage the situation with that ass.

Cherokee slowly walked away making sure each time she switched her shorts rolled up her cheeks a little higher.

I'd be willing to bet $100 he's looking right now.

She briefly turned around to see if she could catch him stealing a glance at her backside. Little did she know Bushwick was a step ahead of her. He already knew the game and turned his back is soon as she began to walk away.

Damn, he didn't even bite. Alright this shit is not going as planned. He should've been all up on me by now. I mean what's really going on when I can't even pull a little nigga like that?

Cherokee went back in the house to regroup. From what she noticed Kweeta usually spent around an hour and a half at the gym. That was pending she didn't pop into a few shops afterwards. Then she could be gone much longer. Whatever the case Cherokee figured she better make her move now just in case midget boy decided to mention the fact that she stopped by and fucked up future visits. She needed to pull him in her world before that happened. Before she realized it, damn near an hour had passed. She was taking a major risk seeing as Kweeta could come back home at any moment but she was desperate.

Think fast, what can you do to get him over here?

She glanced around the room looking for something, anything to give her an idea. Her eyes focused on the laundry basket. She grabbed a pair of socks and folded them together in a knot before taking them to the bathroom and putting them in the toilet. She flushed the handle several times causing the water to overflow. She glanced in the mirror as she hiked the shorts further up in her ass.

I gotta clean this mess up afterwards. This shit better work. If this nigga don't take the bait this time I know he got to be gay.

She quickly made her way back across the street this time tapping Bushwick on his shoulder catching him off guard.

"Damn girl, you scared the shit out of me." She was beginning to annoy the hell out of him.

"I'm so sorry. I hate to bother you again but I was wondering if you knew anything about plumbing."

"Nah, I can't help you with that."

The corners of Cherokee's mouth turn downward.

"That's a shame. I was really hoping you could help. I have water flowing everywhere."

She waited to see if her damsel in distress act was going to work.

"I don't know what I'm going to do. I don't know how to make the water stop." She turned facing towards the house giving Bushwick the full view of her ass.

Suddenly it dawned on him. This was the chick that Austin was smashing.

Damn homegirl thirsty as fuck.

"Why don't you call a plumber?"

"I did try a few people but no one could get to me immediately. And silly me, I don't even own a plunger."

Bushwick shook his head in disbelief. He knew where she was going with this but she was a damn fool if she thought she was getting him up in her house.

"Hang on I think we have a plunger in the house."

"That's so sweet of you Bushwick. Could you bring it over and show me how to use it?"

Oh hell naw! That's the oldest trick in the book. This thot ain't about to mess up what me and my baby girl got.

"Imma go get it but you are on your own after that."

"Ok, I guess I can figure it out."

Cherokee followed behind Bushwick as he headed to the front door. Just as she was about to step in behind him he stopped her.

"I think it's best you stay out here."

***

"Ain't that the bitch that was fucking your friends man?" Laronica asked as she eyeballed Cherokee making her way back across the street.

"Yeah, what the fuck is she doing coming from my house?"

Kweeta had finished her work out early and picked up Laronica on her way home. She cruised down the street and watched as Cherokee switched her way back to her property. She then pulled in the driveway shut off the engine and jumped out.

"Do you think that hoe was over here trying to mess with Bushwick?"

"We 'bout to find out."

"Hey baby," Bushwick greeted her. "What's up Laronica?"

"Hey Bushwick," Laronica replied, anticipating some tea about to jump off.

"Did I just see Cherokee leaving from over here?" Kweeta asked.

"Yeah that was her. I didn't let her up in the crib though if that's what you wondering."

Kweeta's Spidey senses immediately started tingling. Cherokee was the type of hoe that you didn't leave your man around. Even if he was faithful she was the type a bitch that would press until he let his guard down.

"That hoe look like she was wearing a pair of panties. What the hell did she want?"

"Came over here to introduce herself since we never met."

"Since when is that her top priority?"

Bushwick through his hands in the air. "I don't know. I was out here detailing my car and she came over here talking about nice to meet you and asking how we like the neighborhood so far. That was it. She went on her way then came back talking about she had water leaking from somewhere and wanted to know if I knew anything about plumbing. I told her she needs to call a plumber."

"Oooh, that sneaky bitch!" Laronica screeched. "She needed a plumber alright. More like she needed you to come lay some pipe." She knew she was being messy but it felt good to have the heat off her relationship for a change.

"Uhh uh, what the fuck is she sniffing around here for? I'm about to check this hoe right now."

"Kweeta…" Bushwick called out but it was too late.

In a flash Kweeta had turned on her heels and was behind Cherokee before she could make it to her front door.

"What's good Cherokee?"

"Oh shit! Hey… Hey Kweeta? What's going on?"

"What the hell you doing coming from my house?"

Cherokee's heart began palpitating as she eyeballed Laronica walking up behind Kweeta.

"I was just stopping by to see how you were doing. Your fiancé told me you weren't home so I told him I'd come back later."

In the mist of telling her boldface lie she forgot she had the plunger in her hand.

"So what's the plunger for?" Laronica interrogated.

Before Cherokee could reply Kweeta cut into her.

"Yous a muthafuckin' lie! My man told me you was over there all up in his damn face. Asking about a plumber. Bitch, let me explain something to you, you don't have any business at my house when I'm not there."

Cherokee's throat began tightening up. Yeah she was from the hood, but her gut told her that she was no match for Kweeta. Still, she figured she'd better not show fear and play the shit off.

"Girl please, nobody's after that little Chihuahua you got over there. I just had something in my toilet and needed a plunger."

"You 'bout to have my foot in your ass if you keep snooping your thirsty ass around my crib."

"Yeah bitch, we know your type. You like fucking with married men," Laronica barked.

She had no dog in this fight but seeing as she had to deal with the many side chicks that Elroy subjected her to, she was ready for some action.

"Whatever, a queen doesn't waste her time with birds."

She was just about to walk away and give them her ass to kiss when Kweeta snatched her by the back of her hair.

"Come here bitch!" Kweeta flung her to the ground.

Cherokee let out a screech that could be heard two blocks over. "Stop it! Get your hands off of me."

Kweeta kept her promise and cocked her foot back and squared it dead up Cherokee's ass. Cherokee's attempt to fight back was met by blows to the back of the head from Laronica. She managed to wrestle her way to her feet and began swinging wildly, connecting a blow to the side of Kweeta's face.

"Get off me you crazy bitch!"

Kweeta was momentarily stunned by the lick. The next time she looked at Cherokee she had fire in her eyes. "That's all you got hoe?" She gritted her teeth and lunged after her, striking her in the mouth causing her lip to bleed.

"Help!" Cherokee yelped, her teeth now stained crimson red.

She turned to make a run for it and Laronica gave chase, snatching her by her lace frontal, tearing out some of her edges as the glue lifted. This sent Cherokee into a rage. The frontal flapped about on her scalp as she dove on Laronica.

"You want a piece of me bitch!"

Cherokee was beyond outdone. She'd let these rats knock her off her square and pull her into a street brawl.

"Get off my sista hoe!" Kweeta grabbed the plunger and cracked it across Cherokee's back.

"Umph!" She went down with a thud.

"Baby stop!" Bushwick yelled as he approached the women. He tried to grab Kweeta but she dodged him.

By now several of the neighbors were gawking nearby.

Laronica snatched the plunger from Kweeta and mashed the cup into Cherokee's face. "Suck on this bitch!"

"Ewwww!" One of the neighbors called out.

Cherokee knock the weapon from Laronica's hand and wiped the shitty residue from her lips.

"Stop fucking watching and help me! Somebody call the police!"

Bushwick was doing his best to hold back Laronica. Meanwhile Kweeta was on Cherokee's ass like flies on shit.

"Whoop that trick!" Old lady Thomas called out.

"She has it coming! Give her what she deserves!"

"That harlot tried to take my husband also!"

Cherokee couldn't believe what she was hearing. The neighborhood had turned on her. She managed to deliver a body blow to Kweeta that had little impact seeing as Kweeta towered over her petite 5'2 frame. It did however slow her down and give her time to make a break for the front door. Once she was inside she frantically searched for the wearabouts of her cell phone. Not only was she calling the police, she was pressing charges against these savages. Cherokee stopped to listen. She forgot about the water overflowing from the toilet. She stepped around the corner to be met with her guest bathroom totally flooded and had begun seeping into the carpet in the adjacent room.

"Fuck!" Cherokee ran to grab some towels in an attempt to save her $8,000 carpet.

Her plot to make a move on Bushwick had totally back fired. She could call the police later, right now she had bigger issues to deal with. Could this day be any more fucked up?

Once the show was over everyone went back inside. Kweeta and Laronica looked at each other and laughed. They hadn't double teamed a bitch since high school. Kweeta realized that no one was worth risking her going to jail, especially when she'd just preached to Bushwick about his temper. However, Cherokee tested Kweeta's gangster by thinking she was going to pull the same shit with her as she did with Zan. The truth of the matter was part of that ass whooping was payback for how she did her girl. This would be the last time she would get into a physical altercation but it damn sure felt good while it lasted.

****

Chapter 34 - Bounce Back

"That's awesome bae."

"I know right? I gotta admit a nigga was scared for a minute."

"Now please don't mess this up."

"Are you kidding me" Getting off with probation and community service, that's a slap on the wrist for how shit could have turned out considering I had priors. Not to mention my dumb ass was trying to sell to lil' white kids."

"Yes! The Lord was truly in your corner."

"Tell me about it. I really do feel like this was fate. I've always wanted to work with kids so getting this job at the Boy's and Girl's club was right on time."

"Aww bae I never knew that."

"Yeah it wasn't something I really shared. I just feel like if I had some positive role models there for me when I was growing up I might not have turned out the way I did. My parents sat their sorry asses in the crack house a few doors down from my granny and never came to see about me."

He began choking up as he recollected his childhood.

"I always had to fend for myself anyway I knew how. I guess old habits are just hard to break."

Kweeta walked over to him and put her arms around him. "That's all behind you now. And as far as the "way that you turned out," I think you are an amazing man that loves and cares about his family. In my eyes you turned out just fine."

"That means a lot to hear you say that bae."

This was just the break Bushwick needed. Seeing as part of his probation was working with kids, it allowed him the opportunity to gain skills that would prove to be useful in the future. The counseling that was offered on site also helped him deal with his issues of abandonment he'd been dealing with since his parents walked out on him. Now that he'd pretty much cut lose much of the dead weight from fake friends and had took the legal route to securing his own bag, the future was looking bright and he wanted everything it had to offer.

****

Chapter 35 – Letting Go

"Thanks so much for stopping by Zan. I really appreciate you meeting with me," Austin stated somberly.

His bachelor town home was modestly decorated with many of the rooms still empty. His body still wore the scars of his beatdown from Cherokee's cousin.

"It's not a problem. We do need to talk," Zan replied drily.

"How is my baby doing? I wish you would have brought her with you."

"You know she has school. We can set up a time for you to visit with her."

Austin watched Zan's mouth as she spoke. It seemed like ages since he really looked at her and took in how striking she really was. As he admired her beauty he thought how he'd fucked up royally and would do anything to get his family back.

"You look beautiful today."

Zan rolled her eyes. The compliment didn't move her one bit. "Just get to what you wanted to talk about."

"Alexandria please hear me out. I know I fucked up bad. But I love you and Bianca. You guys are my whole world."

Hmph… typical.

"You should have thought about that while you were sneaking around behind my back with that tramp."

"I'm sorry, she means nothing to me. I love you and only you."

As he spoke his eyes traveled to Zan's hand that was reaching inside her purse. She pulled out a Manilla folder and tossed it on the coffee table, cutting him off before he could finish his love proclamation.

"Austin, I want a divorce."

Immediate panic set in. "This is a joke right? We can work this out."

"That's just it, I don't want to work it out. I've put up with your abuse for far too long. That's just a copy. You will be formally served in the next few days. Meanwhile I've packed up the rest of your things. We can set up a time for you to stop by and pick them up."

Austin was outraged.

"So it's like that? I told you that bitch means nothing to me."

"Maybe so, but I can never trust you again."

With that she turned and headed towards the door. Austin walked ahead of her and blocked the exit.

"Zan please, don't let this bullshit tear us apart. I promise I will do anything you want. I'll go to counseling for my anger issues. I can't lose my family," he pleaded.

"I'm sorry Austin I just can't do it anymore."

His face twisted into a scowl from the rejection.

"What if I don't let you walk out of here?" He slammed his fist into the door in an attempt to intimidate her.

"And what? Beat my ass again? Risk going to jail and not seeing Bianca again?" she asked, never flinching.

Austin sucked up his pride and stepped aside.

"Goodbye Austin."

He stood silent in the doorway as his entire world came crashing down and he had no one to blame but himself.

****

Chapter 36 – Hard Saying Goodbye

"I hate that you guys are leaving," Zan said as she helped Kweeta pack the last few boxes.

"It was fun while it lasted but we just decided Beverly Hills is not the place for us."

"I can understand that, It's not for everyone."

"It's crazy, before I got this money I always dreamed of living here. I thought it was going to be like living in a fairy tale. Especially from where we came from. Once I got here I learned that wasn't the case. A few of the people were cool but most of them didn't want us here. Being surrounded by people who are so entitled, people who look down on others and judge them because of what they don't have or where they come from is sickening. Not to mention the pressure of this shit damn near tore me and my man apart. But through the grace of God, true love persevered."

Kweeta's eye's became misty as she thought about all she and Bushwick had gone through.

Zan looked off in the distance. Her thoughts were of her failed marriage and how Austin was the embodiment of everything Kweeta just described. She'd found a true friend in Kweeta and vice versa. Although she hated to see her leave she shared in her happiness.

"So how many days before the wedding?"

"Less than sixty!" Kweeta squealed. "I can't believe it's almost here. That reminds me. Would you like to be my maid of honor?"

"But… what about your sister? Won't she be upset."

"Meh… she might. She'll get over it. I never offered her quite frankly, seeing as her and my mama didn't want me to marry Bushwick from the beginning."

"I would be honored but I have to decline. I think your sister would be hurt if you didn't ask her."

"You're probably right. You can still be a bridesmaid though."

"Now that I can do!"

"And Bianca can be a flower girl."

"I'm sure she would love that."

The women embraced. If Kweeta got nothing else from Beverly Hills at least she gained a friend.

EPILOUGE

Bushwick And Kweeta – The couple moved on to the affluent neighborhood of Baldwin Hills. Even though they were still amongst the wealthy, it proved to be a more welcoming environment. Bushwick continued his education in child development. He took Kweeta up on her offer to help him start his own business. Together they started the Stewart Center. A full service community center for underprivileged youth in Watts and the surrounding area. Through his connections from the center he was able to connect with one of the top producers in the hip hop industry. Bushwick signed with After Math Records and went on to drop two top ten singles on the Billboard charts. Kweeta went on to follow her dream of opening a braiding salon smack dap in the center of Hollywood. Her establishment was such a success that she eventually opened two more locations. The wedding was pushed back due to Bushwick's schedule. However, when the pair did tie the knot it was the social even of the season, being picked up by BET.

Zan – Divorced Austin and is currently living her best life. She followed in Kweeta's footsteps and moved out of Beverly Hills. She found a home in the same neighborhood. She's currently working on opening her own real estate office. Bianca and Bugatti remained friends

Austin – Despite it being a year since the divorce was finalized, he's still in denial that Zan actually left him and took half of everything. He still refuses to seek help for his abusive ways. He's currently back on the dating scene, searching for Zan in every woman he meets.

Cherokee – The bank seized her home for the nonpayment of back taxes. She eventually learned her lesson from messing with married men. As of yet her acting career still hasn't taken off. She eventually settled down with a drug dealer and had two kids. Despite being totally dependent on him, this was the quickest way to secure the lifestyle she was accustomed to without having to work. Let her tell it, she's living her best life.

Sedrick – Still living in the hood. Once word got out about how he betrayed Bushwick most of their mutual friends stopped dealing with him.

Bernisha and Laronica – Both took jobs working at Kweeta's salon. Laronica finally stopped chasing her husband once he admitted that he's been miserable for the past ten years and was leaving her for his side chick. Bernisha finally stopped being bitter and eventually found herself married to a man that adored her. Both of them would go on to apologize to Bushwick and fully accept him into the family.

Until Next Time

Midnite Love

If you have enjoyed this book please consider leaving a review. To the readers and fans your support is greatly appreciated.

CPSIA information can be obtained
at www.ICGtesting.com
Printed in the USA
LVHW111839120319
610380LV00001B/21/P